Once Upon a Royal Christmas

Once Upon a Royal Christmas

Robin Bielman

TULE
PUBLISHING

Acknowledgments

Love and thanks to my wonderful writing friends and supportive family – I couldn't do this without you.

Huge thanks to Meghan Farrell and the Tule team. You guys are awesome and I love working with you.

Special thanks to my editor, Sinclair Sawhney, whose notes were spot on, kind words so appreciated, and emails ones I'll always keep. Thank you to Cynthia Shepp for helping me whip this book into perfect shape. One day all those comma rules will stick in my brain! Maybe. ;)

Thank you to CJ Carmichael for sharing the Bramble House with me, and to Kathleen O'Brien for sharing the Courier and giving me the scoop on Emmaline.

Hugs and kisses to my Sisterhood of the Traveling Crown girls – Samanthe Beck, Hayson Manning, Jane Porter, Roxanne Snopek, Kate Willoughby, Sarah Hegger, and Dani Collins! You magnificent seven are all kinds of awesome and I'm so grateful for your princess support. You all rocked the crown!

And lastly, giant hugs and thanks to my amazing readers and the Main St. Marietta and Tule VIP groups. From the bottom of my heart, I appreciate you taking the time to read my stories and am grateful for your support. You guys are the best!

Oh! One last thank you to Scott Eastwood, for being my inspiration for Prince Theo. :D

Chapter One

ROWAN PALOTAY WALKED down Court Street, her grip tight on two dog leashes in one gloved hand and two more in the other. The wet sidewalk did nothing to slow her four-legged friends. The light falling of snow didn't either. She should be used to the pace, but while she loved these animals, she didn't love her situation. And so she maybe dragged her feet every morning.

Her circumstances were of her own making, however, so she shouldn't take it out on the furry cuteness trying to get to the park sooner rather than later. That was the thought that went through her mind on every walk, and like she always did after the mental reprimand, she quickened her steps.

One of these days, she'd get over her monumental mistake, get a chance to restore her reputation, and prove herself a top-notch news reporter. Maybe.

Hopefully.

Things would get better soon. They had to. Rowan kept hope and faith in her pockets, as well as in her heart, and refused to give up. Ever.

She let out a breath, the puff of air floating in front of her face before disappearing. Snowflakes clung to the needles of pine trees, and the smell of the evergreens reached her cold nose. She loved wintertime in Marietta. And come nightfall, holiday lights would glow throughout town in a kaleidoscope of colors. Christmas in her hometown reminded her there was good in the world. That wishes could come true.

"Hey now," she said as her pooch posse tried to fall out of formation. They may be leading her, but she was in charge of this stroll. If they sniffed even a hint of hesitation on her part, it became a free-for-all. She'd learned that the hard way her first few weeks of dog walking.

She tugged on the leashes and the dogs straightened out. "Good boys."

Oliver glanced over his shoulder at her, and she'd swear the dog winked. The white Samoyed was the most playful of the bunch. To Oliver's right was his brother, Twist, named specifically so the dogs' owners could yell, "Oliver Twist" and get them both to come. Sundance, a happy Chow Chow with a wooly, burnt-red coat strutted alongside Oliver's left. And on the other side of Sundance was Buddy, a Siberian husky, and Rowan's favorite. She was a sucker for blue eyes.

True story.

Okay, stories.

But that was the past and her future was all about independence and playing by the rules. Working hard and reminding everyone she was still the same girl people could count on. Sometimes, omitting the truth just accidentally happened. Nothing Rowan did was premeditated. If anything, she flew by the seat of her pants rather than plan. It felt more honest that way.

Unfortunately, not everyone agreed with that philosophy.

Live and learn, her mom liked to say once she'd realized stubbornness ran deep in her daughter's veins and Rowan had to find things out for herself. She had professional L&L status now, which still didn't always translate to making the best decisions.

She liked to consider herself a work in progress.

"Whoa. Where's the fire hydrant?" All four dogs yanked on their leashes at the same time, the silver bells attached to Sundance's collar chiming louder. Rowan had no choice but to stumble after them since their combined weight beat hers.

Lifting her gaze, she discovered the reason for their excitement. She'd been so lost in thought she hadn't noticed the tall, broad-shouldered man walking toward them. He wore a black winter coat, olive-green slacks, and black dress shoes. He carried himself with confidence, so the black beanie on his head only slightly deterred from the polished look. With the gentle snow flurries, she couldn't see his face clearly yet, but her heart rate sped up nonetheless. It had to be him. She'd heard he arrived yesterday. Had rented the entire Bramble House B&B for the month of December.

What was he doing out for a walk this early in the morning? And didn't he travel with a bodyguard or something? Not that he had to worry in Marietta. The worst that would happen to him here were a few marriage proposals.

And four dogs eager to jump up and lick his face.

Which was what happened while she was still stuck on studying him rather than trying to veer the dogs out of reach.

"Oliver Twist! Buddy! Sundance! Down!" Her command fell on deaf ears as the dogs' leashes tangled while they introduced themselves to the stranger. They didn't jump on the locals. Not usually, anyway. She couldn't blame them at the moment. Prince Theodore Chenery smelled really good, delicately exotic and deeply enticing.

Now that they were closer, she knew it was indeed him. She'd googled him when she learned he was coming to town.

Only a few people knew of his visit, but his anonymity wouldn't last long once the town got wind of his presence.

Speaking of wind, a cold gust blew her hair into her face, making it difficult to see for a moment. She lost precious seconds in her effort to get the dogs to heel, giving them time to wrap their long leashes around her legs, then the prince's. This was not happening. Why, oh why was this happening? *Oomph.* She bumped into the prince while she tried to untangle herself. The more she tried to undo, however, the more she seemed to make it worse.

"I'm so sorry," she said, not meeting his eyes. She was sure she'd find them blazing with annoyance. As far as first impressions went, she was failing in spectacular fashion.

He'd never want to talk to her again after this. Her first—and most likely only—opportunity to meet royalty, and four dogs slobbered all over him.

She reprimanded the dogs again with a sterner voice.

Come on, guys. Cooperate here!

To his credit, the prince had yet to say a word. Probably because he was so taken aback. Thank goodness there was no one else around to witness this debacle. Not that Rowan embarrassed easily. Nothing much ruffled her. But with her reputation already in the gutter, the last thing she needed was to add further tarnish to her image.

Sure, everyone still loved her because family and friends didn't turn their backs on each other, but she wanted their respect back.

Christmas miracles still happened, right?

"Oh, hey!" she admonished. Oliver, the little dickens, somehow got between her legs and her balance teetered. With her hands still firmly clutching the crisscrossed leashes, she couldn't put her arms out or grab onto the prince's coat for purchase. She swayed backward, but the prince wrapped his arm around her waist, saving her from falling on her butt.

Their eyes met. His were ocean blue. The light falling of snow had stopped, and she could see them crystal clear.

She quickly looked away. "Thanks."

He didn't reply. Was he sick and lost his voice or something? She didn't like silence. Much preferred someone yell or rant or talk her ear off. Tell her in no uncertain terms that she had no business walking dogs.

The dog leashes were in such a jumble she had no idea how to extricate herself from the mess. Then she remembered the one and only command that never seemed to fail her.

"Sit!"

All four dogs stopped loving on the prince and sat. Relief washed over her. "Staaaay," she added, and kept repeating it as she performed several acrobatic moves in order to untangle the leashes and free herself and the prince.

Once she had them sorted, she let out a breath. "Sorry about that," she said again, this time meeting the prince's eyes as she spoke the apology. She sincerely meant it and hoped he saw that.

His amazing blue eyes were filled with amusement.

Was she supposed to curtsy and address him formally or something? He didn't know she knew who he was, although given his movie-star good looks and international reputation with women, most females young and old knew who he was. And with the recent passing of his mother, he'd been thrust into the limelight even more.

Since he remained quiet with his lips in a tight line, but slightly curved at the corners, she racked her brain for the right words to say. "Are you laughing at me?"

She bit down on her lower lip. Those weren't exactly the words she'd planned to say. They'd just spilled out without thought. Story of her life. "I mean…"

6

His mouth curled up a little higher. Yep, he was definitely amused by her. And would he say something already? It took a lot to frustrate her, but this man was doing a great job of it.

"Your Royal Highness," someone said from Rowan's left.

Rowan turned her head to find her boss, Emmaline, stepping out of her car. Ro hadn't even heard her pull up to the curb.

"I'm sorry I was late picking you up," Emmaline said.

"No worries," the prince said. "I've enjoyed the fresh air this morning."

He had?

"I'm happy to hear that." Relief sounded in Emmaline's voice as she glanced from the prince to Rowan with worry evident in the creases on her forehead.

Rowan was still on Emmaline's shit list. As the owner and editor of the Copper Mountain Courier, her reporters' actions reflected on her. Several months ago, Ro had been given a piece that was supposed to set her career on fire. Instead, she'd crashed and burned. She was lucky Emmaline kept her employed with The Pet Corner column. *There's not much that can go wrong with animals*, Emmaline had told her.

Emmaline, looking professional and poised, her hair in its usual French twist with a few gray hairs at the root, joined them on the sidewalk. The dogs sniffed around her, but nothing more.

"Good morning," Ro said.

"Good morning. I see you've met His Royal Highness, Prince Theodore Chenery of Montanique."

"That depends on your definition. These guys"—Rowan glanced down at the dogs—"were very excited to introduce themselves, so we really hadn't gotten a chance ourselves yet."

"Your Royal Highness, this is Rowan Palotay. She writes a small weekly column in the newspaper."

The description really tanned Rowan's hide. She was better than a small column and especially unhappy that the story the paper had planned on the prince had gone to her coworker, Marly, instead of her.

Rowan gave a small nod of her head. "It's nice to meet you, Your Highness."

"You as well," he answered cordially.

"I hope you enjoy your time here in Marietta, and I'm sorry to hear about your mother's passing."

"Thank you." His attention never wavered from hers, sending a little shiver through her.

"Okay, well, I should get these guys to the park. Have a nice day," she said to the prince and Emmaline. "Let's go boys." She didn't like being around Prince Theo knowing the newspaper story wasn't hers. If she never ran into him again, that would be fine by her.

Twist, Sundance, and Buddy were ready with tails wagging. Oliver, however, had one more gift for the prince. He lifted his leg and peed right on the prince's pant leg and fancy black shoe.

"Oliver, no!" Rowan pulled on his leash but the damage was already done.

The prince looked up from the dog, his shocked gaze colliding with hers. She darted her eyes to Emmaline. Big mistake. If looks could kill, Ro would be dead.

"I'm super sorry. I don't know what came over him. I'll come by the B&B later and pick up the pants to have them dry cleaned, and then do whatever needs to be done with your shoes."

Buddy barked. Then Sundance. The dogs were beyond ready to hightail it out of there. So was she. Mortification no doubt had her cheeks redder than Rudolph's nose, not to mention sweat trickling down her sides beneath her layers of clothing.

"Apologies again. For everything," Ro added. Then she took off down the sidewalk before any other disasters struck. Or worse, Emmaline fired her.

The start to the day could not be any worse. "Oliver, you are a very bad boy." He looked over his shoulder and gave her the look. The *sometimes-I-screw-up* look. "Yeah, yeah, I know the feeling."

They got to the empty park, and Ro took them off leash so they could chase down the tennis ball she'd brought in her pocket. The treats in her other pocket were the sure way to get them back on leash.

Should she tell Oliver's owners what had happened? No.

It reflected poorly on her skills as a dog walker, didn't it? And she needed this gig to help pay her bills. Lawyer fees had wiped out her savings, and she refused to take any more money from her parents. Her brother, Nick, had already been more than generous as well, and she planned to pay him back every cent.

Rowan, you are keeping your mouth shut.

If only she remembered that more often.

LATER THAT DAY, Rowan dodged a snowball with a big grin on her face. Even two against one, she'd yet to be hit. Granted the boys were ten and eleven, but they were athletic. And had told her with smug little faces that they'd win this fight easy-peasy. That had sealed their fate. Didn't they know she had an older brother who'd taught her to throw a ball—all kinds of balls—from the time she could chase after him?

She hid behind the big pine tree in front of the Bramble House B&B. She'd be sure to let the boys get one good shot in before they were finished, but until then, she gathered some snow into her gloved hands and made another ball. The sun had broken through this morning's dark sky and only a few clouds lingered above. Sunlight slanted through the tree branches, the glare making it difficult to see until she blinked a few times.

Her focus immediately landed on the person she'd been waiting for. She dropped the snowball, jumped out from behind the tree, and hurried to catch Prince Theodore on his way up the shoveled walkway to the bed and breakfast.

He turned his head at her approach, his gaze darting around as if he were looking to see if she had company of the four-legged variety with her.

"Hello, Your Highness. No worries. It's just me this time." She stepped beside him and looked up. He stood at least half a foot taller than her five feet six inches. He'd changed his pants and ditched the beanie. His dirty-blond hair was neatly combed.

"Miss Palotay."

A little thrill raced down her spine that he'd remembered her name. "I'm here for your pants and shoes."

His eyebrows arched up.

"From earlier, sir." It felt weird calling him 'sir' when she knew they were the same age, but she'd read that was one of the appropriate ways to address him. "I promised to stop by so I could take them to be cleaned?"

Out of the corner of her eye, she noticed the two boys, side by side, wind their arms to launch snowballs at her. She turned and waved her arms in a crisscross formation. *Hang on. Don't throw those yet.*

Too late. Big, round, well-packed snowballs—the boys were great at making them—came hurling toward her. Or rather, they came hurling toward the prince. Rowan had a split second to react. She spun around and jumped in front of him, taking one snowball to the middle of her back and the other to her shoulder. The double impact caused her to lean forward.

The prince reached out, but Rowan righted herself before he made contact.

"Gotcha!" the boys called before running across the street to Bramble Park.

She'd been gotten all right. Even though she wore her quilted down parka, she winced at the direct hits. This definitely called for some hot chocolate from the Scott's Christmas tree farm later today.

"You okay?" the prince asked.

"I'm fine," she said, pressing her shoulders back and raising her chin. "I've been hit with hundreds of snowballs."

"I'm not surprised."

"Excuse me?"

"You strike me as good target practice."

Rowan had no idea what to make of that comment. What a rude thing to say to someone who'd—"I just saved *you* from getting nailed by two snowballs and that's what you say to me? Kind of insulting, don't you think?"

"I didn't—"

"You don't even know me."

"I—"

"And for your information"—she almost said "bucko" but caught herself—"it's an honor to have been hit by so many snowballs growing up here. You don't get snow where you're from, so you wouldn't know." He came from a small state along the Mediterranean coastline known for its beaches and yacht-lined harbor, and where the sun reigned supreme year round.

"May I speak now?"

"If you must."

That earned her another arch of his brows. She'd probably be arrested for speaking so disrespectfully to him if they were in Montanique. But this was her home turf and he didn't get to say whatever he pleased. Manners went both ways no matter who you were.

"I meant it would be fun aiming for you."

She crossed her arms over her chest. That still sounded kind of harsh. Even though she *was* fun. "As opposed to aiming for…?"

"Anyone else."

"I'm still not sure what—"

"It was a compliment, Miss Palotay."

She shifted her feet. Okay, so maybe this meant he wasn't holding this morning's incident against her. "Call me Rowan."

"Call me Theo."

"Really?" She'd called him that in her head, but out loud was something entirely different.

"It's what my friends call me."

"Are we friends?"

"You *are* wanting in my pants."

She threw her arms up in the air. He wasn't serious.

"*What?* I do not."

"You don't want to take my pants to be cleaned?" His calm, casual tone irked her. Rowan bet nothing ruffled this man, or gave him pause. Confidence and poise rolled off him like a summer breeze in the middle of winter.

"That's not what you said. You said I wanted *in* your pants."

"You must have misheard me." The small, entirely too charming, curve of his lips told her she had not misheard him at all, and he enjoyed teasing her.

Two could play that game. "That's too bad. I'm very good inside men's pants." She gave him a flirty smile before twisting around and starting up the walkway to the entrance of the B&B. "Let's hurry and grab your trousers, please," she said over her shoulder. "I've got a date I need to get ready for."

She absolutely considered the bathtub and her book a date.

And under no circumstances would she allow herself to think about what it would be like to go on a date with a visiting prince.

Chapter Two

THEO STOOD AT the large front window of the bed and breakfast and watched Rowan walk away. He wasn't quite sure what to make of her. Most women unfamiliar with royalty could hardly string two sentences together when he was around. She, on the other hand, had been completely unaffected by him.

Certainly less enamored than everyone else he'd met since arriving in Marietta. Which wasn't to say the townspeople weren't warm and friendly. They were exceptionally welcoming, but each of them had had a starstuck twinkle in his or her eyes.

Not Rowan. Her big blue eyes conveyed passion and fervor without a spark of infatuation.

And no one had ever talked to him the way she did. She'd gone toe to toe with him, treated him like a normal person. Which must be the reason why he'd teased her.

Then she'd teased him back.

He appreciated it.

He also appreciated this small town, with its history, charm, and snow-covered streets and mountains. It wasn't his first time to the U.S. He'd been to New York and Los Angeles, but never anywhere in between. Never to his mother's hometown of Marietta, Montana. He glanced at the large Christmas tree beside him, aglow in red, green, and gold. It was one of four decorated trees in the Victorian house.

His mom had left home at eighteen for a summer abroad and never returned. On a beach in Montanique, she'd met the newly crowned king, and they'd fallen in love at first sight. They married six months later, much to her parents' objection. According to his mom, it was worry, disagreement, and an unintended slight that had broken the bridge between her and her parents. His grandparents hadn't attended the wedding, though they'd been invited. After that, they'd had very little contact.

But she'd never stopped loving them or teaching the values they'd taught her to her own children. Theo's older brother, Otis, could take or leave their mother's stories about her childhood, cowboys, and the West, but Theo shared in his mom's affection for her past. They often watched old westerns together, and he never tired of listening to her stories of rodeos, snow days, and fishing with her dad.

Outside, Rowan disappeared from view as daylight slowly drifted away. Theo rubbed the back of his neck, sat on the brown leather couch across from the fireplace, and let his eyes drift shut. His mom had led an amazing life before passing away six weeks ago from a ruptured brain aneurysm.

If a woman's worth was measured in admiration, than his mother far exceeded anyone else. She'd given her heart and soul to the people of their province. Theo missed her every day, but he found happiness each day, too, because while her life had been unfairly cut short, she'd left a legacy he was proud to be a part of.

"Tell me again why we had to make this trip now instead of in the spring or summer?" Hawk asked, walking into the room and taking a seat across from him. Theo had hoped to give his bodyguard the month off, but the king insisted Hawk accompany him. That didn't mean his friend had to tag along everywhere he went. In fact, Theo had given him instructions to do his own thing.

"Not feeling the Christmas spirit?"

"You know I hate the snow." Born and raised in Arizona, Hawk wouldn't know a snowshoe from a snowboard. Not that Theo had much experience in cold temperatures either. He'd actually frozen his ass off earlier. But meeting his maternal grandparents for the first time couldn't wait.

"Take off for home," Theo said. "We'll keep it between us." He'd met Hawk five years ago when he was on security detail for an American pop star on a concert tour in Europe. Hawk was quietly looking for a change. Theo needed a new bodyguard. They'd made it official when the singer's tour ended.

"And suffer your father's wrath when he finds out? No thanks."

The king did have an uncanny knack for uncovering secrets. Since he and his brother were young, their father had picked up on every coded message and undisclosed activity. Otis blamed Theo, saying Theo couldn't lie if his life depended on it.

"I'm betting you can find some willing company to keep you warm while we're here." Hawk had mentioned "snow bunnies" a few times since learning of the trip here, and he didn't have any trouble meeting women. If his muscular frame and angular face didn't do the trick, his smooth talking did.

"I may just do that. Speaking of company, a beauty just walked out the door."

Theo shrugged.

Hawk laughed. "Like you didn't notice. She's a spitfire, too."

Long, dark brown hair, full, rose-petal pink lips, and a quick wit. He may have noticed a few things about Rowan Palotay, but it didn't matter.

"I don't think my fiancée would appreciate me giving attention to another woman." Although he already had, hadn't he? Baiting her with the cocky attitude he'd mastered in his early twenties, but more recently retired.

"You're not engaged yet."

"True." And he didn't want to be. At least not to Princess Elisabeth. The recent discovery that Otis and his wife were unable to have children had put extra pressure on Theo to produce an heir sooner rather than later. Since Theo's choice of female company didn't usually meet with his father's approval, dear old dad had decided to take matters into his own hands.

Theo and Elisabeth were friends. They'd traveled in the same circles for years. Shared an occasional drink and conversation at royal affairs. She was smart and kind, but there was zero romantic interest on either of their parts. No spark whatsoever. Obliged by royal duty, however, they both understood the situation and joked it could be worse. They could hate each other.

His father planned to announce their engagement as soon as Theo returned home. *If Mom were still here, this wouldn't be happening.* But it was. And because Theo didn't want to cause his dad any additional pain since losing his wife, he'd agreed to an arrangement that would strengthen the monarchy and bring joy during this time of sadness.

Was it unfair? Yes. Otis had married for love, but since their mom's passing, their father wore his grief for everyone to see and made no secret of his heartache. In conversations with his dad, Theo got the impression the king wanted to spare Theo's heart by having him marry out of obligation, not because he couldn't live without his bride-to-be.

Theo pushed to his feet. "I'm still not used to the time change, so I'm going to take a short nap before I head to my grandparents' house for dinner."

"You want me to drive you there?"

"No. I've got directions."

"See you later, then," Hawk said, scooting closer to the fireplace.

Ninety minutes later, Theo drove onto his grandparents' property. The long driveway had been cleared of snow, leading him to wonder who kept the road passable. Located a few miles from town, the houses were set a good distance from the main road and a substantial distance from each other. He kept his speed to a minimum, the car's headlights the only help he had to guide him.

When a small house appeared on the right side of the driveway, his chest squeezed. *His mother's house.* She'd told him about it when describing where she grew up. The cottage had been meant for her to live in—a way to keep her close, but independent. A Christmas tree with white lights sat in the front window, a wreath hung on the front door. He drove a little further until he reached the main house.

For a few minutes, he stared out the windshield at the rustic two-story residence where his mom grew up. Lights blazed from inside, smoke billowed out from the chimney, and a rocking chair sat on the covered porch.

So different from the Mediterranean-style compound he'd grown up in.

Theo could count on both hands the number of times he'd spoken to his grandparents. When he'd called a couple of weeks ago to tell them of his visit, his grandmother had wept, overjoyed with the idea of meeting for the first time.

She'd asked about Otis, but his older brother had commitments and obligations he couldn't rearrange.

With the gift he'd brought from Montanique in his hand, Theo marched up the concrete steps to the front door. Considering the house was over fifty years old, the structure appeared sound. He liked the light blue siding and gray brickwork.

Before he could knock, the door opened, and there stood Rowan Palotay. Her eyes narrowed at the sight of him, her nose wrinkled. Once again, not the usual expression a woman wore when she looked at him. He smiled in return, just before she slammed the door in his face. That was interesting.

People didn't shut doors on him. They opened them. Wide.

His smile grew despite himself. He'd never met anyone who intrigued and confused him in equal measure. What was she doing at his grandparents' house? More importantly, why did she shut the door?

The door slowly re-opened. Rowan stood there, looking fresh faced and...determined. She wore a thick white headband that covered her ears, and her long, chocolate-brown hair was piled on top of her head. A red scarf hung around her neck. His gaze slid down to her thick, white fleece sweatshirt, then lower to gray pajama pants with white stars on them tucked into black, fur-lined snow boots.

"You're early," she said.

"A little." He looked back up. "You're unexpected."

"That's because you're early."

"Shall I leave and come back?"

"That would be ideal. Say in ten?"

And let her off the hook? No way. Not that he had any idea what hook he had her on. "I thought you had a date this evening."

"Change of plans."

"Pajama party?"

She didn't miss a beat. "Something like that."

"What are you doing here at—"

"Theodore?" a woman said from over Rowan's shoulder.

Theo craned his neck to look behind Rowan. His breath caught when he saw the older woman. His grandmother had the same striking blue eyes, high cheekbones, and chin as his mother. "Hello," he said. Suddenly choked with emotion, he couldn't get any other words out.

Rowan stepped back, the door sliding wider, so grandson and grandmother could see each other fully.

His grandmother's gait faltered, hinting at emotion filling her, too, and Theo strode into the house to meet her halfway. She didn't hesitate to wrap her thin arms around him. He returned the hug and held on until she let go. Bringing her hands to his face, she cupped his cheeks. "You look so much like your mother." He did favor his mom, while Otis resembled their father.

Theo smiled down at her. "It's very nice to meet you in

person."

Tears filled his grandmother's eyes as she tucked her arms to her chest, one hand crossed over the other. "It's wonderful to have you here. David and I have dreamt of this moment."

"Me, too."

"We have so much to catch up on. I want to know everything."

He chuckled. "We have all month to get to know each other." One month for him to gather all he could on his heritage and the small town. "This is for you."

She lifted the small gift box out of his hand. As he watched her open the present, a rush of nostalgia hit his bloodstream. He missed his mom more at this moment than at any other time thus far.

"Theodore," his grandmother whispered. She ran one delicate finger over the ring cushioned inside the box.

"It was my mom's. Before she passed, she told me she wanted you to have it. My father gave it to her on their first Christmas." December 25th also happened to be his mother's birthday. The diamond and brilliant blue zircon ring sparkled under the hanging light in the entryway.

"It's beautiful."

"Let's put it on you." He slid it on the ring finger on her shaking right hand. "I know she's always been in your heart," Theo said. "But now you have something tangible of hers, too. Something that meant a lot to her."

"Thank you." She wrapped him in another hug. He enveloped her petite frame. "Ro, sweetie?" His grandmother stepped around him. Theo had forgotten Rowan was there.

He turned to catch a glimpse of her before she left the house without a goodbye.

"Yes?" She leaned around the big wooden door, her pretty face peeking back inside the house.

"Thank you again for coming over so quickly. I don't know what we'd do without you."

"Of course." Rowan glanced from his grandmother to him. "Have a nice dinner."

"Please don't leave on my account," Theo found himself saying without thought. There was a change in the air molecules when she was around that he wanted to continue to breathe in.

"Heavens, where are my manners? Yes, please stay," his grandmother said. "I insist."

"That's very nice of you, but you enjoy this time together." Rowan gave a little wave. "Goodnight." A second later, the door clicked shut.

"That girl is a stubborn one." Affection filled his grandmother's words.

"Does she live far?"

"Just a short walk to the cottage."

"My mother's cottage?" He didn't know why the idea of Rowan living there intrigued him, but it did.

Glancing down at the new ring on her finger, his grandmother said, "Yes."

"She's walking back? Are there bears or wolves out and about?" He had no idea what winter wildlife might be prowling around the snowy forests of Montana, ready to pounce and drag her back to their cave.

His grandmother studied him. "Rowan mentioned meeting you earlier today. I'm guessing she left an impression, but one that has you worried about her surprises me. I've known that darling girl almost her entire life. She's a very capable young woman, if not a little impulsive."

"Is that a no to the bears and wolves?"

"The bears are hibernating. The wolves, however…"

"I'll just see she gets home safely then. Be right back." He hurried out the door without waiting for a reply. Where he came from, a man didn't let a woman walk home alone.

"Rowan!" *Way to alert those wolves, dumbass.* He jogged to her side.

"What's wrong?" she asked, turning with her arms crossed tightly over her chest. That her teeth weren't chattering in the freezing cold air amazed him. She had no jacket. No earmuffs on her ears like she'd worn this morning.

He took off his wool coat and put it over her shoulders. "Nothing. I just thought I'd make sure you got back to the cottage safely."

Her lips parted, then pressed together, no doubt biting back the urge to say something flippant. "Thank you, but who's going to make sure you get back safely, Your Highness?"

Okay, so he supposed he deserved something a little cheeky from her. "I'll be fine." If he didn't freeze to death first. "And it's Theo."

"What if you slip and fall on the walk back?" She glanced down at his dress shoes. "I'd never forgive myself if you got hurt because you saw me home." Sincerity that surprised him rang in her voice. She was serious, not teasing. "I don't imagine Mediterranean princes have much experience with snow."

"Are you busy tomorrow?"

She frowned. "Sorry, what?"

"Go shopping with me for a pair of boots? I could use your expertise on proper footwear." He bent his head to look directly into her eyes. "Given my limited knowledge with this powdery white stuff." She didn't need to know he'd brought a pair with him.

"I…I can't. I've got a thing tomorrow." She handed him back his coat. "And seriously, I'm good on my own here. You should get back inside."

"I'm seriously walking you home first." He put the coat back on her.

She huffed and resumed walking toward the cottage. "Are you always this annoying?"

"Most women call it charming."

"I'm not most women."

"I'm getting that." He watched her out of the corner of

his eye. Whatever man stole her heart would be in for quite a ride.

They walked in easy silence the rest of the way. Stars sparkled in the sky, and the moon smiled sideways. His fingers were numb, and he couldn't feel his toes, ears, and nose by the time they reached her porch, but he didn't care. He'd enjoyed every second of being out of his element with an interesting—and pretty—girl at his side.

"Thank you," she said, handing him his coat at her front door. Their fingers brushed as he took it. "Holy popsicle stick, your hand is ice cold. Come inside for a minute. I'll give you something for the walk back." She shouldered open the unlocked door, flipped a light switch on the wall, turned a lamp on in the sitting room, and disappeared down a narrow hallway.

Theo admired the tasteful, comfortable surroundings. Traditional brown suede couch with matching ottoman, dark wood side table that held framed pictures, TV and console, fireplace, rich, multi-colored area rug that covered most of the hardwood floor, and the Christmas tree. The tiny white lights he'd noticed when driving by earlier were the only decoration on the fresh pine.

"Here you go. Put these in your hands and they'll be thawed in no time. They're air activated warmers, so you should feel the heat in a minute."

He took the small packets in his palms. "Thank you."

"Sure. Keep your hands in your pockets and they'll be

even more effective."

"Got it. Can I ask you something?" She nodded. "What were you doing at my grandparents' house?"

"Your grandfather pressed the wrong button on the TV remote again and couldn't figure out how to get his program back. I ran up there to fix it for him. He hates to miss *Jeopardy*."

"Jeopardy?"

"It's a popular American game show. Do not, under any circumstances, bet your grandfather you can beat him. He's way too smart for his own good."

Theo slipped his coat back on. "Thanks for the tip. And helping out with things. I appreciate it." His mom was an only child. His grandparents both were, too. The only family they had was friends like Rowan. *You're their family now, too.*

"Your grandparents are amazing people. I'm glad you're getting the chance to know them."

"Me, too." On that note, he needed to hurry back to dinner. Not only because they were waiting on him. But also because the kind, beautiful woman standing a foot away distracted him with increasing potency every time he was near her.

ROWAN STOOD BESIDE her ornament-free Christmas tree and watched Theo through the window. He wasn't at all what she expected. She'd imagined him stiffer and less forgiving, more conceited and less down to earth. Of course he was a gentleman. Princes learned that in Good Manners 101, when they were like four, right? Yet, she got the sense his manners came naturally, rather than being taught.

Once again, her thoughts veered to the Courier and Marly getting the story on the prince instead of her. Ro adored Marly. They were friends even though they were complete opposites. Marly was serious, quiet, delicate. And ethical to a fault. At least Rowan thought that a slight imperfection. She was in the minority, of course, but sometimes breaking the rules came naturally to her. It wasn't that she *planned* to break them. It just happened. Put a check in the bad manners column.

Rowan knew Marly would write a good article.

But it wouldn't be as good as Rowan's. How could it be when Rowan had the inside track? While she and Theo had walked back to her cottage, ideas had fired through her mind like crazy. His story was about more than being a prince. It was about family. His relationship with his grandparents and the town his mother grew up in.

Rowan's feet had been glued to the hardwood floor while she watched Theo and his grandmother meet for the first time. She'd been unable to look away, feeling the love Bea Owens had for her grandson like they'd spent hundreds of hours together. Not ten seconds. The warmth and affection radiating off Theo had been equally palpable. Rowan paid attention to people, and an immediate connection like that was rare.

Special.

The perfect story angle to make hearts pound faster.

Rowan's certainly had, until she realized she was intruding on a very personal moment and had tried to sneak away without notice.

Theodore Chenery had layers she wanted to peel back. If the story were hers she'd get the chance to restore her reputation *and* show off the man, not the prince. *Too late, Ro Lo. There's nothing you can do. The interview isn't yours.* God, it stung to still be punished.

When things stung, she rose to the challenge. *Don't even think about it.*

She kicked off her boots, padded to her bedroom in her socks, and flopped onto her bed. Picking up her cell phone, she thumbed the phone number to her best friend.

"Hey, you," Cassidy said after the first ring.

"I'm in trouble," Ro said in lieu of a greeting. She and Cass were like sisters and formalities weren't always necessary. Actually, as soon as Cass married her brother, Nick, they'd be sisters-in-law as well as best friends.

"Again?" Sympathy and warmth came through the phone line.

"Probably."

"Probably?"

"It's a prediction."

"Ro, if you're not in trouble *yet*, then it can be avoided."

Rowan rolled over onto her side and stared at the half-finished painting of a horse drinking from a mountain lake. Last night she'd been unable to fall asleep, so she'd gotten out of bed to work on something to gift her parents for Christmas. "That's true in theory, but you know how I hate when I'm told I can't do something I want to do?"

"Yeeesss." The extra-long pronunciation was Cass's way of reprimanding her without actually having to scold her.

"What if I wrote my own story on the prince? Something—"

"No. And in case I wasn't clear. No. N. O. No."

"So that's a yes?"

"*Ro.*"

Rowan flopped over to her back for dramatic effect even though Cass couldn't see her. "It's just—"

"What did Emmaline tell you? She said if you step even the tiniest bit out of the lines she's drawn for you, then you're out. No more writing for the Courier. No letter of recommendation when you want to move on. Is that what you want?"

She was silent for a minute, bothered by some recent thoughts that she chalked up to small bouts of doubt. "I don't know what I want." She'd put aside her love of art to focus on writing, but what if that had been the wrong choice? What if the universe was trying to tell her something?

"You made yourself a promise—wait. What do you mean you don't know what you want? Since when?"

"Since The Mistake." Rowan had committed one of the worst crimes a reporter could be found guilty of—not identifying herself as a reporter. She hadn't meant to leave that little detail out, but she'd gotten caught up in her charming, blue-eyed political subject, and it had honestly slipped her mind.

"Then why is the story on the prince bothering you?"

Good question. Was it because Rowan *was* still a reporter and hated losing out on a story sure to garner a lot of attention? Was it because she saw writing something honest and amazing as the only way to redeem herself?

Or was it because she wanted to spend more time with the handsome prince?

"You're right. I'm being stupid."

"You're not stupid. And it's okay to be confused sometimes. What you need is a distraction."

"When are you getting here?"

Cassidy laughed. "I miss you, too. We'll be there in a little less than two weeks. Your brother is taking me to the ball. You're going, right?"

Talk and plans for the Inaugural Christmas Ball had been in the works for months. The Daughters of Montana—women with ties to the early history of Marietta—were planning the event in the grand ballroom of the historic Graff Hotel.

"No. I don't think so."

"Why not?"

"No date." And no plans to jump back in that pool anytime soon. Not unless someone swept her off her feet.

"You'll be our date," Cass said sweetly.

"My brother does not want me tagging along with you guys. But thank you." Rowan rolled off the bed and walked into the kitchen. She pulled two frozen waffles out of the freezer and put them in the toaster. While they cooked, she grabbed the peanut butter and a banana.

"You don't even need a date. I'm sure there will be lots of single people who attend with friends. Come on. When was the last time you got to wear a gown?"

"Ten years ago. Prom. And you remember how well that went." Her date had gotten drunk and thrown up all over her pale yellow dress. Which had triggered Rowan's gag reflex. She shuddered just thinking about it. To this day, she refused to eat pasta with any sort of cream sauce. "Besides, I've got a maid-of-honor dress to look forward to."

"True. But this is Christmas, Ro. Magic happens at Christmas time. Please just think about it a little more."

Rowan sighed loud enough for her best friend to hear. "Fine."

"Thank you."

"Can't wait to see you."

"Likewise. Be good, okay?"

"I'm always good," Rowan answered before they said their goodbyes.

The toaster oven dinged. She loaded her waffles with

peanut butter and sliced bananas. Carrying her plate to the couch, she settled in for some television. When she saw headlights pass by the front window a couple of hours later, she hoped dinner had gone well for Theo and his grandparents.

Then she forbade herself from thinking about Prince Charming for the rest of the weekend.

She was *almost* successful.

Chapter Three

MONDAY MORNING'S DOG walk was far less eventful than Friday's. Rowan wasn't sure why that didn't make her happier.

She stopped at her parents' house to have a cup of coffee with her mom after that. The first words out of her mom's mouth? "Did you know there's a prince in town? Bea Owens' grandson is here. He's a prince." Her mom's excitement was cute. Everyone knew the story of Ashlyn Owens, so there was no need to repeat the prince part.

After telling her mom about her conversations with Theo—in which her mom's hand flew to her heart at least five times—and then making her mom promise to keep it to herself, Rowan went home to shower and dress for her appointment with Emmaline. Her boss had left a voicemail this morning asking Ro to stop by the office.

"Emmaline?" Rowan said, knocking and pushing open Emmaline's office door at the same time. "Hi."

"Come in and have a seat," Emmaline invited from behind her desk. "I'm just finishing an email."

Rowan sat in the high-back chair in front of Emmaline's

desk. She'd comfortably sat in this exact spot hundreds of times, but since The Mistake, it was no bed of roses to be called in to talk. Still, she smiled at her boss, because the thorns in their relationship were all Rowan's fault and she still respected Emmaline a heck of a lot.

Emmaline looked directly at her as she shut her laptop. "The prince wants you."

"*What?*" Fired. He wanted her fired because of the whole dog fiasco. She'd also called him annoying, hadn't she? And she might have been too forward with the 'in the pants' thing.

"Prince Theodore would like you to interview him."

Oh. "He…he would?" she asked, surprised.

"Yes." Emmaline folded her hands atop her desk. "He says he's happy to be featured in the Courier, but only if you're his reporter."

"What did you tell him?"

"I told him yes. Now here's what I'm going to tell you— you will not engage in any unnecessary behavior or at any time question him off the record. You're to make him understand everything he says to you can be used in your story. Things will be kept professional at all times. Is that clear?"

"Crystal." Rowan hated that Emmaline thought she still deserved a lecture. She didn't make the same mistake twice.

"You've got until the first."

"Thank you," Rowan said appreciatively as she stood. "I

promise I won't disappoint you."

Emmaline smiled. Rowan gave one back and left quickly before Emmaline changed her mind. Jingle bells and jamberry jam, she had the story! A chance to make things right and earn back the respect of her peers, her family, and her friends.

On her way out, she stopped at Marly's desk for a quick chat to make sure they were good. "We're good." Marly said.

Her feet lighter, Rowan stepped out onto the shoveled sidewalk. Was it her or did the snow look whiter? Today's blue sky brighter? She thought about going right over to the Bramble House B&B to see if Theo was there so they could pin down some days and times to get together. Instead, she did an errand. He probably expected to hear from her today, so she'd wait until tomorrow to get in touch.

For some reason, she didn't want to do what he expected.

That didn't count as unnecessary behavior, did it? Shoot. It probably did. She tucked her scarf tighter around her neck and strode toward the bed and breakfast.

She turned the corner onto Bramble Street, not liking the unfamiliar quivers crowding the pit of her stomach. The second she saw the action at the park, though, the unwelcome ache abated.

Theo, a small group of boys—including her snowball opponents—and a tall, good-looking man she didn't recognize, were playing football. Rowan's eyes tracked Theo as he

ran for a pass. For a guy unaccustomed to chilly temperatures, the prince seemed unbothered by the frigid, uneven
snow under his feet.

He had on jeans, a long-sleeved Rugby shirt, and the
same black beanie he'd worn the first time she met him. The
throw missed him by several feet. He fetched it. Ruffled the
small quarterback's hair as he handed the ball back. As if
sensing her gaze on him, he turned his head, smiled, and
waved.

She waved back and walked closer to the action.

"Let's take five," Theo said, still looking at her. She was
still stuck on him, too. He looked just like one of the guys,
albeit more handsome than any man she'd ever met before.

"Your Highness." She gave a little nod.

"Rowan." The way he said her name made it feel like
eighty degrees outside instead of forty.

"I guess we'll be seeing more of each other. Thank you
for the vote of confidence. I'm not sure what I did to deserve
it, but I'm going to save my questions for more important
topics."

"Sounds good." His gaze slid away from her to
acknowledge the man coming to stand beside them. "Hawk,
meet Rowan Palotay. Rowan, this is my friend and bodyguard, Hawk."

Now that he was closer, she recalled catching a glimpse
of him when she'd picked up the prince's pants and shoes.
"Hi, it's nice to meet you."

Hawk's large gloved hand swallowed hers in a hand-shake. "You, too."

He had a vibe very different than Theo, a tall, dark, American vibe. "You're from the States?"

"I am."

"So you decided some football in the cold air and snow would be fun for our ocean city prince?"

Both men studied her thoughtfully, like she'd said something worth noting. They shouldn't read anything into it. For the next few weeks he *was* her prince. Professionally speaking.

"Actually, I dragged him out here when I heard the kids playing," Theo said.

With the schools just a few blocks away, the park often ended up being an after-school playground and a chance to let off some energy before heading home for homework and chores.

"I hate the snow," Hawk said. To emphasize his point, he kicked up some powder.

Rowan laughed. "This little vacation sucks for you then."

Hawk grinned with good humor and mischief evident in his expression. Oh, the single women of Marietta were going to love him.

"Hiya, Rowan," Mack Sheenan said. The sweet, adorable preteen handed her the football. "I've got to go. Will you take over for me?"

She palmed the ball. "Sure. Say hi to your dad and Harley for me."

Swinging her attention back to the double dose of male hotness, she found Theo and Hawk staring at her like Joe Montana had magically appeared behind her. She smiled inwardly. JM was her favorite professional football player. When she was little, she loved him because his last name was the name of her state, and that had stuck with her into adulthood.

Anyway, these two studs obviously had no idea she had mad skills with a football. Thanks to her high school football star older brother, she knew how to throw, catch, and intercept a football like the powder-puff champion she was. The snow underneath her boots could prove a little challenging, but she never backed down from an opportunity to surprise people.

"Looks like I'm your new teammate, Your Highness. Let's do this." She shouldered her way between the men and marched toward the boys jogging in place to keep warm at the scrimmage line.

"She's serious," Hawk said from behind her.

She hung her messenger bag and scarf on a tree branch and joined the group. After a quick lowdown on the rules and where the end zones were, she turned to Theo. "Want me to quarterback?"

"Uh, sure." By the stupefied tone of his voice, he was still stunned she had game.

"Cool." She led the huddle. Led them to score by running in a touchdown on the third down. Fist bumping a prince was definitely one of her favorite things ever.

Theo wrapped his arms around two of his young teammates' shoulders as they took to the defense. "I know you guys have got this, so where do you want me?"

"You're good with kids," she whispered to him as they lined up in the side-by-side formation the boys suggested.

"I like them."

She knew that from the googling she'd done on him. Theo wasn't only a prince, but a pilot who gave countless hours to flying kids and their families to his family's private island and resort. The destination was a free vacation spot for children suffering from illness or tragedy.

"Twenty-seven, thirty-four, seventeen hike!"

Rowan pulled her gaze off Theo and placed it back on the game. No way would she be able to get by Hawk to tag the quarterback, so she took off in pursuit of one of the young receivers.

"Man down!" one of the boys shouted not two seconds later.

She whirled around to find Theo sitting in the snow. Oh no. Her breath caught in the back of her throat. *Please don't let him be hurt.*

"It's just a twisted ankle," he was saying as she reached his side.

"I'm really sorry. I didn't mean to trip you," sweet Hunter Zabrinski said.

"Hey." Theo put his hand on the boy's shoulder as Hawk helped the prince to stand. "You didn't do anything wrong. My footwork is to blame. I was so busy trying to copy your awesome moves that I fouled up. I do believe I'm done playing for today, though."

Theo exchanged one-armed hugs with the boys. "Thank you" and "that was fun" were said numerous times. Rowan grabbed her things and hurried over to hook her arm around Theo so Hawk didn't have to carry all his weight. By the way the prince limped, he'd more than twisted his ankle.

His beautiful blue eyes met hers when she ducked and put his arm over her shoulders. "How bad is it?" she asked.

"Not bad."

"You always wince when it's not bad?"

Hawk chuckled.

Theo scowled at him. "It's a little overly sensitive because I broke it six months ago."

"I guess grace doesn't come with the royal package," she teased.

"My royal package is better than anyone else's. Trust me."

Hawk barked out another laugh. Rowan's mind went straight to the gutter. *Show me.* Whoa. Put on the brakes, Miss Hard Up. She was not allowed to think anything inappropriate with regards to the prince. From now on, if her thoughts ventured to Theo naked, or half-naked, or even flashing a smile, she'd think about scary clowns instead.

"You know what I mean," Theo grumbled. His grouchy tone was cute. And indicated he was definitely in more pain than he wanted to let on.

"I don't think she does," Hawk offered, hilarity in his voice.

"Some things are better left to the imagination." She did not just say that. She pressed her lips together. Maybe they didn't hear her.

"Not this time," Theo said, regaining his composure and sliding her a look that was impossibly sexy.

"Okay, enough, you two," she said as they reached the steps of the B&B. "Let's check out this injury, and then I'll be on my way."

"Thanks for helping get me here, but I'm fine." He removed his arm from her shoulders and opened the over-sized wooden front door for her. Hawk kept a hold of him until they reached the couch in the sitting room.

The scent of gingerbread filled the air, and Rowan's stomach grumbled. Eliza, manager of the inn with her husband, Marshall, baked the best gingerbread cookies.

"Be that as it may, I need to take a look." She knelt beside him, carefully pushed his jeans up to his shin, and removed his sock and shoe. She didn't know when it started, but she felt responsible for him. "It looks a little swollen."

"I'll grab some ice," Hawk said.

Theo didn't take his eyes off her as she cradled his foot in her hand. "How did you break it?" she asked.

"Water skiing."

"I've broken my hand and two fingers."

"At the same time?"

She shook her head. "Different times, different hands. Both when I was young. In fact, your grandmother was the nurse who took care of me in the ER. I remember our first meeting vividly. She was much more sympathetic than my parents were."

"Really? Why?"

"Because I broke my hand punching Billy Pruett in the face." She grabbed the blanket from the arm of the couch and put it on the coffee table. With a gentle touch, she put Theo's leg atop it.

"Thanks," he said, relaxing against the couch cushions. He pulled off his beanie and ran his fingers through his hair.

Was his hair as soft as it looked? *Scary clown. Scary clown.*

"What did Billy do to deserve a punch in the face from a young Rowan Palotay?"

"He was bullying my best friend Cassidy, calling her names and telling his friends things that weren't true. He wouldn't listen when I asked him stop."

"Seems to me a good reason to hit someone."

"Yes, well, my mom and dad were of the *use your words* philosophy. They were proud of me for standing up for my friend, but wished I used different means. Billy and I were both suspended from school for the rest of the week."

"Did he bother your friend again after that?"

44

Rowan smiled. "No."

"You're a good person to have on their team." The compliment, combined with his warm gaze, was her cue to get her butt out of there pronto.

She stood at the same time Hawk entered the room with an ice pack. "I'll check in with you later."

"About that." Theo put the ice on his ankle. "I've been interviewed plenty of times and wondered what your angle was. My main reason for being here is to get to know my grandparents and this town."

"I know," she said. "So how about I play tour guide slash reporter slash"—she hesitated—"friend. I've lived here my whole life and have known your grandparents almost that long."

"Okay," he said simply.

"But everything we say to each other is on record. Nothing is off limits. If we can agree to that now, we don't have to worry about any miscommunication later."

"Agreed."

"Great." Getting that out of the way lifted a weight she hadn't realized sat on her shoulders. "Take care of your ankle and I'll start thinking about things for us to do. I'll touch base with your grandparents, too. I don't want to interfere with anything they might have planned for you."

"Thank you. I'm sure they'll appreciate that." He was looking at her weirdly, so she said a quick goodbye to him and Hawk and hurried out the door.

She welcomed the crisp, clean air into her lungs with a deep breath. Theo made her nervous, no doubt. But what prince wouldn't make a country girl a little restless? Those eyes, that mouth, the broad chest, were a royal combination unlike any other. He only held power over her if she let him, though. He brushed his teeth just like every other person. Put on his shoes one foot at a time.

Prince Theo was just extraordinarily normal.

And she could handle him and her story.

Probably.

THE FIRST WORD to come to Theo's mind when he saw the picture in front of him was "unbelievable." The next word was "feisty," followed by "beautiful." He didn't say any of them out loud. He put the car in park in front of his grandparents' house, hopped out, and jogged over to help.

"Hey there, Super Girl," he said to Rowan. "I'll get this side."

She stopped pulling the fresh-cut Christmas tree that was taller than her up the steps and released a deep breath. "Hey."

"So I should add tree delivery to your list of attributes?"

"I didn't realize how big it was when Carson helped me with it."

"Carson?" he asked, wondering for the first time if Rowan had a boyfriend. But if this Carson person were with her, surely he'd be here to help.

"He runs the tree farm on the outskirts of town. Your grandparents were going to head there in the next few days, but I thought to surprise them instead. This year is…" She dropped her head and sat down on the top step.

Theo walked around the tree and got comfortable beside her. He had a feeling she was going to say "harder" given they'd lost their only child. It didn't matter the years and distance that had separated them. He knew the second he'd met his grandparents that they'd never stopped loving their daughter. He also knew his mom wanted her family happy by the life she'd gotten to lead, not saddened.

He bumped his knee against hers. "Did you know I have a Marietta fan club? As my go-to person here, I think that's something you should have given me a heads-up on."

She lifted her chin. Her intriguing, and grateful-he-changed-the-subject, blue eyes sparkled. "I did hear about that. How does it feel to be adored by kindergartners?"

"It's not the first time young ladies have declared their love for me," he teased.

Rowan pressed her lips together, but the corners of her mouth lifted. Against her will, he imagined. "Yeah, I bet. And now that pretty much everyone knows you're here, it's only going to get worse."

"Is that why you've kept your distance the past two days? Strategizing on how to get your story and stay out of the limelight?"

"Actually, I wanted to give you time to rest your ankle. How is it feeling?"

He straightened his leg and made a circle motion with his foot. "Great. It's like I never tripped and embarrassed myself in front of a beautiful girl."

Her cheeks flushed a pretty shade of pink. He didn't think she had a blush in her, given the tough, spirited vibe she gave off, but it pleased him that he was wrong.

"In that case, let's get this tree inside." She jumped to her feet. Wiped her hands down the sides of her jeans.

They proved to be a good team, hoisting the tree into the house and standing it by the window in the front room. That is, until they both let go at the same time. The fragrant pine started to topple before he pulled and Rowan pushed it back to an upright position.

"Okay, who's holding on and who's letting go?" Rowan asked through a chuckle.

"I'll keep it standing," he said.

"You sure?" she teased.

"Grab that metal base thing. Don't worry; I'll get the tree in it." The tree wobbled as Rowan let go, his grip not as secure as he'd thought. In his defense, the tree had a good two feet on him.

"Theo?" She grabbed the tree again. Then, in some crazy tug of war between the two of them, the tree teeter-tottered. "Maybe I should hold on to it," she said.

"No, I've got it," he countered.

"I don't think so," she argued.

"Really, I do," he confirmed. Pine needles were dropping like snowflakes during a blizzard with all the back-and-forth movement. And the tree's girth was proving to be quite problematic, but he had it. If she'd just let go already.

Rowan cracked up—a loud and joyful life-is-good laugh that fit her dynamic, upbeat personality to a T. The sound echoed off the walls. Rang in his ears like an unforgettable song. He made it his secret mission to hear it more often.

"Okay, okay," she said, her laughter falling away. "I'm backing away from the tree."

"Excellent."

"So, I'm guessing you've never put up a tree before. Probably had staff that did it for you?"

Theo heard Rowan shuffling about, but he couldn't see her around the bulk of the tree. "What gave me away?"

"Your very clever use of the term 'metal base thing.'"

"Clever *is* part of my charm."

"Have you ever decorated a tree?" she asked, ignoring his comment. The sound of her voice came from the vicinity of the floor this time.

"That I have done, yes. My mom made it a tradition. We had a private tree in the family quarters. Every year, she would put on holiday music and we'd decorate it."

"That's nice. I've got the base ready," she said near his feet. "If you can lift the tree for a few seconds, I'll slide it under the trunk."

"Let's do it on three. One…two…three…" He did his part, heard the scraping of metal on the hardwood floor as he tried to keep the tree balanced, and blindly fit it into the base.

"Shoot. We need to try again. It's going to be a tight fit."

"No worries. I'm an expert at getting into tight spots," he said, his voice a little husky.

Rowan cleared her throat. "I walked right into that one, didn't I?"

"You did." That she called him out on his flirting made her even more appealing. This attraction to her was damn inconvenient. He couldn't act on his feelings. Not when he promised his father he'd marry Elisabeth. In a month's time, his engagement would be worldwide news.

"All right, Your Highness, let's do this." It didn't go unnoticed that she called him "Your Highness" whenever she needed to put some distance between them.

Which meant she wasn't as unaffected by his nearness as she wanted him to believe.

He wished that didn't please him so much.

Chapter Four

THEO STARED AT the Christmas tree ornament in his hand, at a loss for words. People had shown him kindness his whole life. He chose to believe it was him and not his royal bloodline that warranted attention. But the reality was, he could never be sure.

He felt sure now.

As he stared at the white dog with a football in his mouth and "Theo" written across the dog's chest, he realized this gift was the realest thing he'd received from anyone outside his immediate family. He lifted his eyes to Rowan.

She sat across from him in his grandparents' house, the fireplace glowing behind her, the Christmas tree to her right. She wore jeans, a form-fitting, emerald-green sweater, and a wide smile. "It's kind of perfect, right?"

"It is. Thank you."

"The first honor is yours," his grandmother said, indicating he should stand up already and put the ornament on the tree.

When he'd helped Rowan with the tree yesterday, he hadn't imagined sitting here tonight carrying on a tradition his mother had stamped on his heart. Holiday music played on an old-fashioned turntable. Boxes of ornaments were open and waiting to be hung.

He had no idea if it was the right thing to do, but he went with the strong compulsion to thank Rowan again. On his way to the tree, he bent and kissed her cheek. "Thank you," he whispered.

To say the brief, innocent contact made him crave more would be an understatement. Her soft skin, her feminine scent, the hitch in her breath, all conspired to make him glutton for punishment.

He'd only known her a week, spent a handful of hours with her, yet he liked her more than he'd liked anyone else in a very long time.

He aimed for the center of the tree and hung the ornament by the red ribbon attached to it.

"David, you go next," his grandmother said to his grandfather as Theo turned around.

For the next thirty minutes, they shared stories, laughed, and Theo drank his first Irish coffee. The easy way the four of them got along made him very happy he'd decided to visit during the holiday.

"Um, no," Rowan said out of the blue, removing the purple-and-gold ornament ball he'd just placed. "You can't put that there."

"Why not?"

"Because there's another one like it right there." She

nodded toward a similar ball.

"There are three different types of ornaments in between." He'd done this enough times to know ornament etiquette.

"Still too close." She reached up with the ornament in her hand, stretching her arm as high as she could. His gaze fell to her waist, where a patch of smooth, creamy skin was now visible. Too quickly, she lowered her arm. "There. Much better."

"You're messing with me." In more ways than one.

"What? No, I'm not," she said defiantly, but he heard the goad in her voice. She picked up the last two ornaments, handed him one.

He watched her hang the gold-and-white star.

Then he hung his gold-and-white star right next to hers, close enough that their points touched.

She eyed him. He eyed her back, hoping she got the message. They'd draped well over a hundred ornaments. Ornaments his grandparents had accumulated over fifty years of marriage. This was his way of leaving evidence of his friendship with Rowan. If he'd had glue on him, he would have bonded them together for future Christmas's when they were far apart.

"You're too much, you know that?"

He frowned. "Too much what?"

"Just too much." She stepped around him to help clean up the empty ornament boxes.

ROBIN BIELMAN

"Anyone for another Irish coffee?" his grandfather asked.

"Yes, please," Rowan answered. "And could you make mine a double?"

"I'll help," Theo said, following his grandfather into the kitchen. He wasn't sure what had just happened with Rowan, but he had the feeling she'd appreciate his absence for a few minutes.

"Your mother loved drinking coffee when she was a teenager," his grandfather said, sharing more private thoughts. Theo was grateful his grandparents seemed to very much enjoy reminiscing about their daughter.

"She loved it as an adult, too." Theo watched his grandfather mix heavy cream, sugar, and coffee liqueur into the topping for the coffee. "But she never let my brother or me have even a sip when we were growing up. She said it would stunt our growth."

His grandfather laughed. "Your grandmother used to tell your mom it would keep her hair from growing. I told her while I loved her mother very much, I respectfully disagreed, and so it became our little secret that we drank coffee together."

Theo leaned his elbows on the granite countertop of the kitchen island. "She loved to fish with you, too."

"Did she tell you she always threw them back?"

"No."

"She hated the idea of any living creature dying before its time. We caught a good fifteen-pound lake trout once. It

54

pained me to toss it back, but when she looked at me with those blue eyes of hers, I was always toast."

"She had my father wrapped around her finger, too."

"I'm happy to hear that." His grandfather added a couple of tablespoons of Irish whiskey and a spoonful of brown sugar to each mug, stirred. "What about you? Anyone special waiting back home?"

He wanted to say Elisabeth was special because if he thought it enough while on this trip, hopefully he'd believe it when he got home. But there would be time to find out what made her special later. Right now, he couldn't think past their friendship or wrap his head around the idea that sometime next year he'd be married.

"Actually, as soon as I return home, my father is announcing my engagement."

Surprise clouded his grandfather's gray eyes. "Who's the lucky girl?" He poured the strong, dark coffee into the mugs.

"Her name is Elisabeth."

A noise sounded from over Theo's shoulder. He turned to find Rowan hopping on one foot as she entered the kitchen. "Sorry. Just me banging my foot on the corner of the wall." She looked affectionately at his grandfather. "Did you move the walls? I know you've been working out."

The older man grinned as he added an enormous dollop of the whipped cream concoction to one of the mugs. "This one's the double," he said pushing it toward the edge of the counter.

Rowan stopped bouncing and stood across the kitchen island. She wrapped her hands around the ceramic cup. "Thank you." Then she pursed her pink lips together and lightly blew on the hot beverage.

Theo choked back a groan. Everything this woman did had his body reacting in some way or another.

She lifted her gaze, her long lashes sweeping up. "So engaged, huh? Congratulations."

"I'm not engaged yet, but thank you." The words were uncomfortable when spoken to Rowan. Not because he didn't want her to know, but because he would have preferred she hear the news directly from him.

"Wait. I'm confused." She rested her elbow atop the counter and cupped her chin in her hand. "You haven't asked her to marry you yet? I thought I heard you say your dad is making the announcement."

"He is. It's an arranged marriage, so I won't be getting on bended knee." The thought bothered him more than he imagined it would. He'd never spent any time thinking about a proposal. Hadn't pictured the perfect girl. Not yet. But something about a romantic start appealed to his core belief that marriage should be based on love. Admiration. Finding the one person he couldn't live without.

"Wow. People still do that? That's kind of rough." Rowan said, breaking into his thoughts with genuine curiosity. That she wasn't teasing him meant a lot. Could she tell this arrangement bothered him?

Not that there was anything he could do about it. Once his father had made a decision, he didn't change his mind.

"Occasionally."

"Occasionally what?" his grandmother asked, walking into the kitchen.

"Theo's engaged to be engaged," Rowan said, her tone over-the-top perky. "At his father's request. Or, rather, insistence, I guess."

His grandmother put her hand on his arm. She looked him straight in the eyes. Hers were earnest, searching. The back of his neck tingled as he waited for questions he didn't want to answer.

But to his relief, his grandmother turned and said, "Who wants another piece of pie?"

In that moment, he knew leaving Marietta would be harder than he'd imagined.

"THANKS FOR THE ride," Rowan said with a smart-aleck tone. She couldn't help it. "That walk would have wiped me out." She hopped out of the passenger side of Theo's rented SUV thinking she'd say goodbye to him at his window. She found him standing outside the car, instead.

"What are you doing?" she asked.

"Seeing you to the door."

"It's like fifty feet away."

He gave a one-shoulder shrug, put his hand on her lower

back, and steered her toward her front door. His manners were ridiculously inconvenient.

Because you like them.

Like *him*.

He's engaged! Almost. So no licking allowed. Liking. She meant liking.

"Rowan, did you hear what I said?"

"Sorry. What?" The warm feel of his palm on her back had completely distracted her from everything but the uninvited thoughts in her head. This increasing attraction to him had to stop immediately.

"I asked if you wanted to finish up the questions you started earlier? I'm not very tired, so…"

"Sure. We could do that." She could absolutely remain professional around him. *Scary clown,* she silently repeated over and over again until she sat on her couch, Theo beside her.

"Can I ask you something?" he said before she had a chance to speak. She nodded. "Why don't you have any ornaments on your tree?"

The tiny white lights made the Christmas tree festive, but without any other adornments, it remained lifeless. "I'm waiting," she said, softer than she'd meant to.

"For?"

Openness went both ways and if she wanted Theo to be open with her over the next few weeks, then she needed to give him the same courtesy. "My own family. I've always thought decorating a tree for Christmas should be about family and love and so I want to wait until I'm married or at least engaged. Like you, my family decorated the tree together every year, and I'd like to follow the same tradition. I think it will be more special if I wait to start until I've got someone important to share it with."

"Is your family still here in Marietta?"

"My mom and dad are. My older brother, Nick, lives in Los Angeles, but visits often."

"Will he be home for Christmas?"

"Yes. He and his fiancée, Cassidy, the best friend I mentioned to you from my childhood, are flying in next week to stay for the holidays."

"Your brother's engaged," Theo stated. Like he was trying the word out for only the second time, which seemed weird, even if his was an arranged thing.

"And he's ridiculously happy about it. He rented a yacht for a week for just the two of them and popped the question one morning by spelling out 'Marry Me, Sid' with buoys in the water."

"Wow. That's impressive."

"Right? But he *was* in the Navy, so he had help from some Coast Guard friends. He brought Cass up on deck, led her to the railing, and when she looked out onto the water, he got down on one knee. They're getting married in May."

Theo stayed quiet, his face unreadable.

"Don't let his romantic gesture get to you, though. My

brother and Cass have something really special. She had a crush on him when we were young, then they didn't see each other for over ten years. He was here in April for a bachelor auction, and that's when they reconnected." She turned her whole body so she faced him, cross-legged, on the couch. "Go."

"Go?" he asked with a frown.

"I've monopolized this conversation way too much. It's your turn. Talk to me, Prince Theodore. Tell me, how long do royal engagements usually last?"

He rubbed the back of his neck, his attention dropping to the floor. "I suppose as long as is deemed necessary."

"Sounds like you can't wait," she said gently.

"Right." Only he meant wrong and she knew it. Being the polite prince he was, though, he couldn't share that truth out loud.

A bunch of new questions stormed through her mind. How well did he know Elisabeth? Did he at least like her? Could they live together before marriage? Was she pretty?

"I was engaged once," she said.

That grabbed his full attention. Even put a little spark back in his electric-blue eyes. "You were?"

Rowan sighed, letting her shoulders fall and her lashes flutter. "His name was Gregory Daniels. We sat next to each other in second grade. He was the first boy to write his phone number on my hand."

The sexy curve of Theo's lips almost made Rowan regret

sharing this story.

Almost.

She focused on the Christmas tree lights. "He asked me to marry him over chocolate milk and peanut butter cookies. I said yes." Gregory's eyes had been see-through blue, and she'd been intrigued by them. Not to mention he could draw a horse and cowgirl better than she could. That had been the moment she'd decided to take art more seriously. "The next week, though, he asked Summer Reynolds to marry him. When she said yes, he dumped me."

"Idiot."

"Thank you."

"No. Thank you."

"I didn't do anything."

He draped his arm across the back of the couch, his hand landing dangerously close to her shoulder. He seemed to weigh his words carefully before saying, "I like the things that come out of your mouth. They make me..." His finger lightly—and briefly—grazed her shoulder before he pulled his arm back. Her body caught fire. God, she hoped he couldn't see his influence on her. "We're friends. Elisabeth and I, so I suppose that's something."

Friends.

That shouldn't make her stomach churn like she'd eaten bad fish, but it did. Which made *her* an awful friend at the moment.

"That's good," she said with a nod. "And you know, everything happens for a reason." Not that she'd figured out why yet. Some things sucked when they happened. Theo's nose-diving eyebrows suggested he agreed with her.

She had a solution for that. Her go-to remedy when a situation bothered her. "Stand up," she said, getting to her feet and grabbing her phone. "Come on," she added when Theo was slow on the uptake.

"Are we going somewhere?" he asked approvingly.

"Nope. We're dancing." She found her Rocky Horror Picture Show playlist. Two seconds later, "The Time Warp" played through the wireless speaker next to her TV. She thought this might be an introduction to the British-American cult classic, given Theo's royal upbringing, but by the look on his face, she hadn't initiated him into anything.

"You've heard this?" she asked.

"Once or twice," he said with a smile so sexy and warm that her skin tingled.

"Why do I get the feeling it's more than that?"

"I don't know." With that darn smile still in place, he stepped around the coffee table so they were only a couple feet apart.

She turned up the volume, and he proved he knew the song quite well as they danced around the room and sang the lyrics. Then they froze, called out "Let's do the Time Warp again!" and showed off the steps while facing each other. It was silly. It was fun. The prince let loose with her, and when she sang along to the lyrics at the top of her lungs, he didn't put his fingers in his ears.

He moved with skill and grace and confidence that were insanely attractive.

Song after song played. They lost themselves to the campy, upbeat rhythms, dancing around the room like they didn't have a care in the world.

Theo unbuttoned the top two buttons of his shirt, then pushed his long sleeves up to his elbows. Rowan stared at the hollow of his neck, wondering what it would be like to put her lips there and breathe him in. Her gaze slid down to the light dusting of blond hair that covered his tan, muscular forearms. What would it feel like to have those arms wrapped around her, keeping her warm on snowy nights?

She spun and gave Theo her back. Staring at the man was not helping to keep her mind off him. And no amount of scary clowns was strong enough to cure her of this crazy prince affliction. It was so easy to be with him, talk to him. Let her guard down with him.

The music stopped and they both collapsed onto the couch.

"Can I get you some water?" Rowan asked.

"That would be great, thanks."

In the kitchen and out of view of the prince, Rowan blew out a breath and fanned her sweater away from her stomach. It wasn't that she got overheated dancing.

Her problem came in the shape of a man with blue eyes, blond stubble on his jaw, and a body made for indecent positions. She couldn't remember the last time she'd been so enamored and carefree with a guy. Theo pressed all her buttons. Something none of her boyfriends had done. But she needed him in order to restore her reputation and gain back the respect she craved. And that meant no more fun and games.

Because that kind of diversion landed a girl in trouble.

Chapter Five

THEO SCRUBBED A hand down his face. Rowan's question shouldn't surprise him. She had done her research. Had brains to go with her beauty. Behind her baby blues lay a one-two punch of curiosity, but also kindness. He studied her from across the coffee table in the sitting room of the Bramble House and decided it would take a very long time to learn everything there was about her. She was a living, breathing adventure wrapped up in a gorgeous feminine package.

"I take it your silence means you don't want to answer the question?"

Wrong. It meant apparently he couldn't do two things at once—talk and look at her. A problem he'd never had with another woman before.

"Sorry."

"Sorry you zoned out on me, or sorry you have no desire to answer the question?" she asked with sweetness in her tone of voice.

Oh, he had plenty of desire. Only it had nothing to do with this interview. He'd asked Emmaline for this, though, so he'd follow through with every one of Rowan's questions even if he could think of a much better way to spend their time together. *You cannot think like that.*

"The former."

Rowan smiled in encouragement and gratitude. *Go on,* the small curve of her lips said.

"You're right," Theo continued. "My mother was extremely conscientious when it came to helping others. She raised me to have an understanding of people's hopes, their insecurities, and their difficulties. And I plan to spend the rest of my life trying to fill the void she's left behind."

"Most people would probably say you already are. Your family's island vacation for children who have suffered in some way is amazing. And that's just one of the philanthropic activities you participate in."

"My mom taught me that caring is a universal language, and I believe that starts with young people. Kids are the key to the future. All the incredible things that are going to happen ten, twenty, fifty years from now, it's going to be because of them. They've got the know-how, but we need to help them along."

"Do you want to have kids of your own?" Rowan brought the tip of her pen to the corner of her mouth as she waited for his reply. The gesture drew his eyes to her heart-shaped lips. In response, her gaze dipped to his mouth.

Then slowly, with undisguised appreciation, she returned her eyes to his. She no doubt saw the same expression in his fixed regard.

Everything seemed to come to a standstill as the magnetic pull between them took up all the space in the room.

Just like it had during last night's impromptu karaoke. After guzzling an entire glass of water to cool the blood pumping through his veins, he'd walked away from her when it was the very last thing he'd wanted to do.

She cleared her throat now, broke their connection first. Her eyes might be somewhere over his shoulder, but awareness continued to make his skin warm.

"I'd love to have children one day," he said after a beat. Preferably in a couple of years, but nothing about his situation with Elisabeth was his choice. His father wanted heirs to the throne now, not later. If Theo were marrying the love of his life, he'd be right on board with that. But since he wasn't, he wanted the chance to bond with Elisabeth before they took such a big step.

"You look…" Rowan paused. Bit the corner of her lip.

He had to stop looking at her mouth. "I look?" he prompted.

"Knock, knock," Eliza said, even though there was no door. She walked into the sitting room wearing a festive Christmas sweater. She seemed to have several and added to the holiday spirit every time she walked into a room. "Mind if I interrupt for a minute?"

"Not at all," Rowan said, sitting taller and pressing her hands into her lap. Theo didn't miss the fact that her full attention on Eliza took the pressure off his question.

"I'm not sure if you've heard about the Christmas Ball," Eliza said, taking a spot on the couch next to him. "But I'm on the planning committee and on behalf of the Daughters of Montana, we'd love for you to attend. The ball is to commemorate the 125th anniversary of the courthouse and is on Saturday, the seventeenth. I've got a ticket for you right here."

He took the offered ticket and read the details.

"Please say you'll join us. It would make our night to have a real prince at the ball," Eliza continued. "Everyone is going to be there."

Theo lifted his head and his eyes locked on Rowan's. "Everyone?"

Eliza glanced at Rowan. "Most everyone, but I don't believe you've bought a ticket yet, have you, Rowan?"

"I haven't. I'm—"

"Is it all right if I bring a guest?" Theo asked.

"Of course," Eliza said, waving her hand in the air. "I'll get you another ticket and you can bring whoever you'd like. And, of course, Hawk is invited as well. I'll leave a ticket for him in his room. Your grandparents will be there; I know that."

"I'll definitely be there, then." His grandparents had put zero pressure or demands on him, letting him set the pace on their time together. This event sounded like a big deal, and he'd like to enjoy it with them. He pictured Bea and David in formal attire, dancing the night away. He'd been cataloging every moment with them since he had no idea when, or even if, he'd make it back to Marietta again. Perhaps they'd visit him one day, to meet Otis and see their homeland. There was a lot Theo would like to show them.

"Wonderful." Eliza jumped to her feet. "I'll let you two get back to business. Thank you, Your Highness."

"It's my pleasure. Thank you for the invitation."

"I saw your grandmother's gown for the ball," Rowan said as Eliza stepped out of the room. "It's beautiful. And your grandfather is wearing a tux. He also ordered a corsage for your grandmother, but please don't tell anyone that. He wants to surprise her. The two of them are still so cute." She twirled a strand of her long dark hair around her finger.

"They are that," he said in agreement. "What about you? You're not planning on going to the ball?"

"No."

"Why not?"

"It really doesn't matter." She fiddled with the notebook in her lap. "Now where were we?"

"Be my date," Theo said.

Rowan stared at him. He wasn't sure if she was happy or put off by the suggestion, so he decided to rephrase it.

"I mean, would you please do me the honor of being my date for the Christmas Ball?"

"You want me to go with you?"

"Yes."

She blinked as if he'd asked a much more serious question, like say, "May I kiss you?" Which, thankfully, he *hadn't* voiced out loud. Damn his one-track mind. He would not be kissing Rowan. He simply liked to be around her. They were *friends.*

"I'm not sure that's a good idea." *True.*

"Why not?"

"Because people will talk."

He shrugged. "People talk about me all the time. But if you're worried about tarnishing my perfect image, don't be. I can handle it." One side of his mouth lifted in a smile.

"Aren't you cute? Thinking you're perfect and I could negatively impact your reputation. I'm pretty sure you've taken care of that all by yourself, what with all the pictures of women I've seen you with. 'Royal Bad Boy' I think one publication called you?"

She'd done a very thorough research job on him. Interesting.

"You think I'm cute?"

Rowan rolled her eyes. "Is that all you heard?"

"No. But you shouldn't believe everything you read in magazines or see on the Internet."

"I don't," she argued.

"So, the ball then. Will you be my guest?" It wasn't the wisest move, asking her to be his date, but he couldn't stop himself. After last night, he wanted to dance with her in his arms. Hold her close. Breathe. Her. In.

"I could go on my own, you know. See you there."

"If that makes you more comfortable, okay." It really wasn't, but he wasn't used to chasing after a date. He also had a feeling she did want to go with him, but didn't like the idea of saying yes too quickly. Rowan Palotay liked to be the one making the decisions.

He'd best remember that and bury his attraction to her.

He hadn't come to Marietta to get close to anyone but his grandparents.

Close.

When was the last time he'd felt truly close to a woman? Let himself relax and not worry about paparazzi or other prying eyes. He couldn't remember. And while the people of Marietta had definitely taken an interest in him, they didn't have an agenda.

"It does," she said softly.

"No problem. It's a date then?"

"Okay." A sudden look of excitement lit her eyes.

"What?" he asked, leaning forward and putting his elbows on his knees.

"You've just upped the ball preparations big time. The committee was already working really hard, but now that you'll be attending, I imagine no one is going to get any sleep until it's over. Eliza has probably alerted everyone already, and I'm picturing party chaos to make the evening outstanding. I'm glad I'll get to see the final result."

"Me, too."

Very glad. Which made him foolish, but he didn't seem to care.

ROWAN HATED CANCELLING her plans with Theo. But worse, she'd planned to continue her work on the mural at the hospital this morning. She *really* hated not showing up there as promised, but in the middle of the night, she'd spiked a hundred and two degree fever that didn't show any signs of weakening. Popping fever reducers every four hours helped in the short term, but her body still ached miserably. She was hot, then cold, her skin clammy, then brittle.

She pulled the blanket tighter around her body and sank deeper into the couch. Outside, snow fell in big, fat flakes, but on the television screen, divers swam in an aquamarine sea as she watched *Into the Blue* for probably the tenth time. If a shirtless Paul Walker couldn't make her feel better, nothing could.

A knock sounded on her door, and she frowned. Since when did her mom knock? "It's open," she called out. Her mom had phoned earlier to say she'd be by with homemade chicken-and-rice soup. It was Rowan's favorite. Her mom rocked.

The person who entered the house, however, wasn't her mom. "Theo, what are you doing here? I told you I was sick." As she sat up, the blanket fell to her lap.

"Hi," he said, gently closing the door behind him. "I

thought I'd bring you something to eat."

Okay, so maybe the devastatingly handsome prince could make her feel better. With his light blue jeans and black windproof down jacket, he looked like he'd stepped out of the pages of a Patagonia catalog. He slipped off his beanie, and she gulped. She wanted to run her fingers through his mussed golden hair so badly.

She sat on her hands.

He stamped his black snow boots on the welcome mat, unzipped his jacket, and hung it next to hers on the wall-mounted coat rack. Ro's mouth dropped open. It must be her fever, because his black, long-sleeved crewneck T-shirt showed off his broad shoulders and slim waist in a way that made her wiggle on the couch. When he turned, the stretchy thermal tee accentuated his muscular chest and flat abs.

Could the guy just once look unkempt instead of hotter than any man had a right to be?

"Thank you," she managed to say, then more clearly, "but I don't think you should be around me. Whatever virus I've got, I'm probably contagious. My fever hasn't broken yet."

"I'll risk it." He placed a large brown bag on the coffee table and filled the couch beside her. His eyes touched every part of her face like he was looking over something important. Valuable.

She felt his exploration all over her body. Tiny tingles that spread a delicious kind of warmth through her.

His gaze dipped to her chest. And holy mother of pearl, the curve of his lips made her dizzy. She'd seen a lot of his smiles, but none like this.

Glancing down to see what had him looking like the best thing since peanut butter, she took in her striped heather grey T-shirt and scrunched up her nose. Of all the shirts she had to be wearing, the one that said *Let's get naked!* with a cartoon banana tossing off its peel was the worst. The skinless banana had a black rectangle over its… private part.

When she lifted her gaze, Theo stayed quiet, but his eyes danced with amusement, reminding her of their first meeting when she'd wanted him to say something. Anything.

"Are you laughing at me?" She'd asked him the same question that morning a couple of weeks ago.

This time, he answered. "Absolutely not. I'm just enjoying the view."

She dropped her chin to take another peek. Yep, he knew without a doubt that she wasn't wearing a bra. Which didn't bother her in the least. She liked her body and didn't mind it being appreciated. So rather than cover up with the blanket like she suspected he thought she'd do, she took her hands out from under her legs and rolled her shoulders back to stretch.

He made a deep, guttural sound, then cleared his throat and grabbed the brown bag. "I wasn't sure what you'd be in the mood for, so I got a few things."

"That was really nice of you, but you shouldn't have."

Theo took out a carton of orange juice and put it on the coffee table before swiveling toward her. His expression turned serious. "You take care of people all the time and deserve to be taken care of in return."

"I don't—"

"You saved me from snowballs, helped when I hurt my ankle." He reached out and brushed her hair off her forehead, his finger delicately tracing her hairline down the side of her face. She melted a little bit. "You gave me hand warmers when I thought for sure I faced possible frostbite, and you surprised my grandparents with a Christmas tree. You've made me feel a part of their lives, and a part of this town, by giving me an ornament to hang on that tree. I can only imagine all the other things you do so, for the next hour, let me take care of you."

Tears burned the back of Rowan's eyes. He was right. She liked, no *loved,* giving, but had a hard time receiving. That he was here and saying such nice things, that he'd appreciated what she'd done, turned her world upside down. Turned her heart into one of those winged cartoon drawings, ready to take flight so it could make its home on his shoulder.

A big part of her wanted to argue with him, but the soft parts inside of her won this time. She stared into Theo's bottomless blue eyes, knowing she was helpless to fight what he offered.

"Okay," she said quietly. "Thank you."

He returned to the task of emptying the brown bag. "Liquids are important and orange juice is rich in Vitamin C, so we've got that along with some flavored waters with electrolytes. Soup is the go-to when sick, so I brought chicken noodle and vegetable." He placed the items on the coffee table in a straight line. "We've also got yogurt, bananas"—he cut her a quick side glance—"and the ultimate fever reducer, cayenne pepper.

We.

He kept saying 'we.'

She didn't know what to make of that.

Wait. "*Cayenne pepper?* I've never heard that before. What do you do with it?"

"Sprinkle it on your food. It helps you sweat out the fever and promotes blood circulation."

"Yeah, because it's hot and spicy. I'm not a fan of hot and spicy."

"No?" Theo asked with a gleam in his eye. "I bet I could change your mind."

Oh, boy. Was it warm in here? Her body on fire, Rowan reminded herself she didn't let a guy get the upper hand, even if she couldn't stop thinking about having his hands all over her body.

"I'll just have a yogurt please, minus the cayenne pepper." All the food was such a lovely gesture, but her mom had made special soup and would be over soon, so Rowan didn't want to spoil her appetite. What little of it she had.

"Is it okay if I put the rest of this away in the kitchen and grab you a spoon?"

"Sure. Thank you. It's at the end of the hall."

She watched him pull a small spice container out of the bag and place it on the coffee table before he gathered everything else up and walked into the kitchen without a word.

If she didn't already feel herself liking Theo waaaayyy too much, this sealed the deal. She could fight against the physical attraction, but getting to know the man on the inside made it difficult not to fall for him a little bit.

It wasn't the first time she'd been smitten with a man who was unavailable. Yes, she'd been misled the last time, but she'd never make the same mistake again.

Besides, everyone in Marietta was smitten with him. In the grocery store yesterday, she'd overheard more than one conversation where women fantasized about Theo. Gushed about him and his good looks and manners.

Cutting herself some slack, she reached over to pick up the spice. Mustard powder. She had no intention of putting *that* on her food either.

Theo seemed very busy in her kitchen, the sound of cupboards opening and closing and the faucet running grabbing her attention. She stood to go find out what he was up to, the blanket falling to the floor, and, *oh, yeah*. All she had on besides her banana T-shirt was boy short panties.

She quickly sat back down and wrapped the blanket

around her waist and legs. She'd been so hot earlier that she'd flung her pajama pants off when she'd gotten out of bed to watch TV.

Noise in the kitchen stopped. A moment later, Theo appeared holding the red ceramic bowl she used for popcorn. "Since you're opposed to cayenne pepper, this is the next best thing," he said, handing her a spoon as he knelt to put the bowl at her feet. It was filled with water.

"My mom used to do this whenever my brother or I had a temperature." He opened the mustard powder and added maybe a couple of teaspoons to the water. "Your feet, malady."

He pushed the bowl closer to the edge of the couch while she lifted the blanket and tucked it around her knees. If her bare legs surprised him, he didn't let on. She, on the other hand, was painfully aware of her lack of clothing with him so close.

"The hot water and mustard powder draw blood to your feet, which also increases blood circulation, and can remedy fevers." He lifted one foot by her heel and placed it in the water, then did the same with her other foot. Her size sevens fit with no problem.

She gave a sigh of bliss at Theo's warm hands and gentle touch. He looked up and their gazes collided. Held. The sound of her phone chirping with an incoming text broke their connection. *Perfect timing.*

Rowan leaned over to look at the screen of her cell. The

text was from her mom saying she'd been held up and would be over in time for dinner instead of lunch. "Love you" and several emoticon hearts followed. Her mom had recently become a big fan of texting and one emoji was never enough.

"Everything okay?" Theo asked.

"Fine." She settled back into the couch with her yogurt, more than ready to concentrate on something besides Theo. "This feels nice. Thank you," she said, wiggling her toes in the hot water.

"My pleasure." He sat back down next her. "What are we watching?"

"*Into The Blue*. We can change it though, if you want. I've seen it several times."

He picked up the remote and scrolled through the guide. "*A Million Ways to Die in the West*. Know what that's about?"

"Oh my God. It's hilarious. It stars Seth McFarlane and Charlize Theron and—"

"Say no more." He clicked to the station where the movie was scheduled to start in a minute. "I'm a big Seth fan. And western movie fan. Growing up, my mom and I would watch westerns all the time. She might have taken to the Mediterranean with ease, but...but deep down, she was still a country girl."

The note of pain in Theo's voice had Rowan putting her yogurt down to squeeze his hand in comfort. "I bet she loved sharing that with you."

Rather than let go of her hand as the movie started, he held on. She'd never thought much of handholding, previous boyfriends not being big on that particular gesture of togetherness. But sitting with Theo, her small hand laced with his much larger one, felt more intimate than kissing some of those bad boys she'd been attracted to in her youth and early twenties.

Soon, Theo's hour of company turned into three. They watched the entire movie, laughing at the same parts, stealing glances at each other at the same time, too. They paused the film twice. Once, so he could take the basin of water into the kitchen, and a second time so he could grab a cold drink and ibuprofen for her. She could get used to this kind of attention.

After the movie, they talked. About family, his love of flying, dogs, stupid things they did as teenagers, and food. He told her about the cuisine in Montanique—lots of fish, vegetables, rice, pastas, and olive oil.

"As soon as I'm better, I'm going to take you for pizza that will blow the taste buds out of your mouth," she said.

"I look forward to it." He stood to leave, glancing out the window where snow fell in thicker sheets than when he'd arrived.

She wrapped the blanket around her body so she could see him to the door. "Thanks for coming over. I'm…I'm glad you did. But you cannot blame me if you get sick."

"I wouldn't dream of it," he answered good-naturedly

before his attention caught on the side table near the coat rack. "Wow." He picked up one of the cards she'd hand drawn. "Did you do this?"

His notice of something so personal made her uncomfortable. She plucked the card out of his hand and put it upside down atop the others. "Yes. I like to make my holiday cards."

He stole another one out from the pile before she could stop him. "They're fantastic. When you said you got arrested for graffiti as a teenager, I wasn't picturing…"

"Something good?" She couldn't believe how easy it had been to tell him about her troublemaking youth. But the nonjudgmental, interested look in his eyes had her spilling things she didn't normally share. And maybe she was trying to give him reasons not to like her because that would be a lot easier than dealing with his friendliness.

"This is more than good. You're really talented."

"It's nothing. Just a hobby." That she loved. When she drew and painted, she forgot about everything else but the artwork.

Theo looked around the room as if searching for more artwork. "Have you done anything larger?"

Yes. "Okay, buddy, enough with the questions. You need to go so I can take a short nap before my mom gets here and wants to hear every detail of our afternoon together. If I tell her." Who was she kidding? Ro told her mom everything.

"Should I stick around to meet her?"

"Only if you want to be trapped here for another two hours and asked a gazillion questions. I didn't get my inquisitive nature from my father."

"That would make me very late for dinner at my grandparents' house, so I'd best be on my way." He slipped his arms into his jacket. "I'll check in and see how you're doing tomorrow. Feel better."

"I will." She had too much to do to be sick. A deadline she had to make even if it meant working all through the night.

"Soak your feet again later."

"Yes, sir."

He smiled. She returned the gesture. Then she discretely inhaled his delicious scent one last time and watched him go, grateful for the gust of frigid air that came through the front door and cooled her overheated body.

A feverish feeling that had nothing to do with being ill.

Chapter Six

ROWAN'S FEVER LASTED twenty-four more hours, which meant she spent Sunday cooped up at home rather than painting. Losing the entire weekend put her way behind schedule, which was why she stood in the main hallway of the pediatric wing of Marietta Regional Hospital at eight o'clock at night, bone tired from working on the mural all day, but determined to get a little more done before she left.

She'd promised to have it finished by the fifteenth—three days from now—and she never broke a promise. Not that she was worried. But she wanted it to be perfect and that meant leaving time to take a step back and give her imagination a rest, then returning to look at the mural from a distance to keep in touch with the bigger picture. This helped her to see if anything looked wonky.

Arms at her side, a drop cloth under her feet, a sponge in her hand, she let out a deep breath. *It's almost there.*

Deer in ballet slippers, dogs decked out in football jerseys, horses wearing cowboy hats, and happy little children all danced across the wall. A sun wore a mustache. Clouds shaped like airplanes dotted a royal-blue sky.

The goal was to boost the spirits of the young patients in the twelve-bed unit and to put a smile on their faces. Rowan had been beyond pleased when her drawing was approved and the hospital administrators had been eager for her to start.

And despite the long day, she'd loved every minute of it. Painting, sponging, and stippling brought out a special energy inside her. She lost herself in the whimsy of her creation and forgot about everything else on her mind. Her hours at the hospital were an escape. Not very many people knew about the project. She'd asked to keep it quiet. This mural was as much a gift to herself as it was to the hospital and the children.

"Thought you might need this," someone with a deep voice said to her left.

She turned to find an attractive man maybe a few years older than her handing her a cup of coffee from the cafeteria. He'd been here as long as she had today, nodding or giving a small smile to her when he walked by. Rowan guessed he had a child in one of the rooms, and her heart hurt for him.

"Thank you." She took the offered drink. "It has been a long day." *For both of us.*

"This looks amazing," the man said, his attention moving to the mural.

"Think it's lively and uplifting enough to entice kids out of bed?" Rowan hoped beyond hope that she'd succeeded in that. Hospitals were miserable, sterile, scary, and devoid of color. But not this unit. Not anymore.

"Absolutely. I think it will definitely perk up even the most sullen or grumpy child."

Was his son or daughter feeling like that? She wanted to ask about his situation, but stopped herself. Sometimes just a simple conversation with a stranger was what a person needed.

"That's our hope."

"Hope no more. You've succeeded."

Rowan smiled. His compliment landed in the back of her throat and it took her a minute to respond. "Thanks. The children who saw it today did seem pleased, but once I'm finished and get this mess cleaned up, that will be the true test."

He cast his nice, but worried dark eyes back on her. God, she could only imagine how painful it must be to have a child sick or seriously injured. "You're very talented…"

"Rowan," she supplied to his trailing off.

"Rowan. I don't think you need to worry. Besides, kids aren't too critical, especially in a place like this."

"Sometimes it's the little things, right?" She took a sip of her coffee. She very much appreciated his small gesture.

"Exactly." He glanced back at the mural. "Nice choice in animals. My daughter loves horses."

They stood side by side and stared at the wall in silence until Rowan said, "What's your daughter's name?"

"Annabelle."

"I'll keep Annabelle in my thoughts."

"I'd appreciate that. Goodnight." He walked away with his shoulders slightly hunched and his gait heavy, as if exhaustion lived in his bones.

Rowan closed her eyes and gave a silent prayer for him and his daughter. Then she gave thanks to the blessings in her life, including a prince named Theo.

HOW MANY DOG walkers did it take to walk four dogs and a goat? *More than one*, Rowan thought to herself while being pulled in different directions the next morning. Seriously, what had made her think adding Pepper to the mix was a good idea? The goat was sweet as could be, but had no idea how to stay in the group. Worse, whenever Oliver got the chance, he tried to get frisky with Pepper… and that was a sight Ro wished could be bleached from her memory.

If she made it through this walk without her arms being pulled out of their sockets, she'd count it as a win. "Sit," she commanded, a little out of breath. The dogs sat. The goat twirled in a circle.

Rowan cracked up.

Which the dogs decided meant, "stand up" because they got to their feet and started down the shoveled sidewalk again.

Pepper looked a little dizzy and actually walked in the opposite direction. This only made Rowan laugh harder. She got tangled in the long leashes and her grip started to slip on the three leashes in her right hand when the sexy voice from her dreams last night said, "Looks like you could use some help."

Her eyes caught on twin shades of tropical blue that never failed to quicken her pulse. "No. I'm good!" she said in between chuckles. "I've got this totally under control."

"Is that…a goat?" Theo asked with surprise and confusion.

"You say that like you've never seen one before." Rowan struggled a bit with the leashes but since Theo's arrival, the dogs had stopped pulling and chosen to sniff and lick his hands as he pulled off his gloves to pet them.

"Not on a leash."

"Count that as another Marietta first."

"I will."

Intrigued by the handsome stranger who had the dogs strangely calmer, Pepper nudged her shoulders between Oliver and Twist to see what the fuss was about.

What the heck? His Royal Highness hadn't demonstrated any of these dog whisperer skills the first time they'd met. Rowan's jaw dropped as Theo bent over to rub the top of the dogs' heads, and they sat there perfectly behaved like he was the master of the universe.

"I've never petted a goat before. What's his name?"

"*Her* name is Pepper."

"Hello, Pepper." He scratched the top of Pepper's head.

"What's with the mad animal skills all of a sudden?" Rowan asked as she took advantage of Theo's calming effect on her charges and organized their leashes.

Theo straightened and his grin showed off very nice teeth that gleamed whiter than the snow around them. "It's called dog treats." He slipped his hand in the front pocket of his pants and pulled out a handful of the soft beef jerky treats dogs loved. "I thought I'd be better prepared today."

How was it the man could look so polished and sophisticated one minute and boy-next-door adorable the next? Both were undeniably sexy and made it difficult to look at him sometimes.

"Good thinking," she said.

"It's a known fact I'm not all good looks."

She rolled her eyes and handed him two leashes. "Well, Smarty McFarly, I guess you can make yourself useful then." In her head, it wasn't leashes she handed him, but her clothes as she suggested much better ways to use him. And let him use her.

Her brain needed a serious time out.

Or maybe she needed to jump back in the saddle and give the dating thing another try. All her ex's *had* been good at using her.

Then deciding she was too smart, too pretty, too creative, or too family oriented for them to deal with. She wasn't sure what that said about the guys she'd been with, so until she figured it out, she'd been on a boy break.

Men suck.

Besides, her job and reputation needed all her attention right now.

"Every one of them?" Theo asked from beside her, the dogs and Pepper walking almost in straight lines in front of them.

Crap. She'd said that out loud. "No, not all of them."

"Phew. I thought I was going to have to slay a few dragons for you while I was here."

"I'm no damsel in distress, Your Highness. I can take care of myself."

The sun peeked out from behind the clouds, chasing away the frigid morning air and raising the temperature a couple of degrees. Or maybe it was a hint of anger brewing under her skin. She didn't need a man. She *wanted* one.

"I've no doubt of that, but sometimes a prince likes to toss out a quip in hopes of making someone smile. Especially when he's not around other royals who would find his overused joke stupid rather than amusing."

Rowan bumped him with her shoulder. "You amuse me very much, Prince Theodore."

Theo laughed. "Touché, Miss Palotay."

"Are you still up for some adventure today?" She planned to take Theo for the pizza she'd promised and show him some of Marietta before heading back to the hospital to work on the mural tonight.

"I'm counting on it," he said, sounding eager, before

they fell into comfortable silence.

It wasn't until after Theo crossed the street back to the Bramble House and Rowan had gotten her four-legged friends to their homes that she realized the prince had sought her out this morning for no other reason than to be in her company.

She wished that didn't make everything inside her go haywire.

THEO PULLED OUT Rowan's chair before taking the seat across from her at the small back table in the Italian restaurant. She smelled like cinnamon and citrus and he'd never inhaled anything so...sexy. She unraveled the scarf from around her neck, unzipped her jacket, and hung both over the back of her chair. Her ivory wrap cardigan had a deep V neckline. Her hair fell in big waves around her shoulders and down her back. He followed suit and removed his jacket. It was that or lean over the table and run his tongue over her neck to see how her smooth skin tasted.

Their eyes met over their menus and stayed fixed like they so often did. Something was most definitely going on between them. She felt the sparks like he did, but they both knew they shouldn't—couldn't—do anything about it.

"Put your menu down. I'm ordering for us," she said. Her voice was a killer combination of rock star and pin-up girl, and it was getting harder and harder for him to ignore the way it made him want to throw caution aside and use their mouths for things other than talking.

He obliged her request and looked around the pizza parlor. Marietta had a charm he hadn't counted on liking so much. Down to earth mixed with country and classic styles that could make even the most diehard city slicker feel at ease. Theo did miss the sleek, modern comforts of home, but this town—he glanced at Rowan—and the people in it, made him forget about being homesick.

When their pizza arrived, Rowan placed a slice on each of their plates. "Ready to be blown away?" she asked.

Her enthusiasm had him willing to like the pizza no matter what. "What am I looking at here?" He picked up his piece and blew on it.

"Uh…" Her focus dipped to his mouth before she gave a small shake of her head and studied her own piece. "This is the sweet potato, bacon, and maple chipotle pizza. I know it might sound weird, but wait until you taste it. It's my favorite pizza ever."

He was always game for anything, so took a big bite. Rowan watched him, waited. "Well?"

"It's good. Really good." He took another bite.

She wriggled her shoulders in satisfaction, then dove into her slice, finishing it quickly before grabbing another piece.

"If you could only have one food with you on a deserted island, what would it be?" Rowan asked, licking some cheese off her finger.

His gaze zeroed in on her mouth, he shifted in his seat. "That's easy. Stocafi."

"What's that?"

"It's cod fish cooked in a special tomato sauce and very popular where I'm from. What about you?"

"Hmm. That's not so easy for me." She put her food down and leaned back in her chair. "I think I'll go with Eggos."

"And those are?"

"You've never had an Eggo? It's only the best frozen waffle ever. I'll make them for you one morning." He raised his eyebrows. "Or evening," she quickly amended. "They're good any time of day. If you had to choose to live without one of your senses, which one would you give up?"

Theo wiped his mouth with his napkin and relaxed in his seat. He'd play this game all day with Rowan if it gave him the opportunity to ask her the question in return. She was no doubt tucking away everything he told her. But so was he.

"Hearing."

"Me, too. If you could bring one fictional character to life, who would it be?"

"Are we talking books or film?"

"Either."

"Harry Dresden."

"No way! You've read the Dresden Files books? Harry is who I would pick, too." She bit the corner of her mouth. "We're two for two. Okay, time travel to the future or the past?"

Theo bit back a smile. He felt like a teenager, talking like this. It was refreshing. Hot. Rowan's curiosity was genuine. The conversations they shared were unlike any others he'd had with women. "The past."

"Seriously?" She huffed. "I have never gone three for three with someone before." She fiddled with the straw in her water glass. "Last one. Explore outer space or the deep sea?"

That she'd played this game with others shouldn't bother him, but it did. He studied her. His answer didn't matter as much to him now as hers did. Given they were in Montana, he took her for a girl who gazed at stars. He loved the ocean. Did he give an honest answer and break their streak or go for gold?

"The deep sea."

"I thought you'd say that."

"And you're an outer space girl."

"The sky's the limit, right?"

"Kiss and tell or never be kissed," the waitress said as she refilled their water glasses. She put her palm to her mouth, then pulled it away and blew him a kiss before she strode out of eyesight.

Rowan chuckled. "I'm surprised she was the first one to do something like that. Every female in here has had her eyes on you."

He hadn't noticed. He only had eyes for Rowan. "Should

we give them something to talk about?"

Her normally expressive face went blank. "No. We shouldn't," she said determinedly, and he had a feeling he'd hit an uncomfortable chord with her.

"I was teasing." Not really.

"I know. But…"

"But what?"

"I'm your reporter and that means behaving with the highest integrity," she said, voice lowered. She took a sip of her water. Despite her wise statement, he found himself staring at her lips wrapped around the straw and thinking about where on his body he'd like to have that soft, full mouth.

"You've done just that, no worries."

"Thanks. Let's finish this pizza and get out of here."

They polished off lunch without further conversation, and twenty minutes later in the privacy of Rowan's car, Theo said, "Kiss and tell."

"Obvs," Rowan fired back. He was fairly certain that meant obviously.

It also broke the tension between them and things returned to normal as she gave him a driving tour of snow-covered Marietta. She talked nonstop about the town, sharing the lowdown on landmarks, Christmas events, and where to grab the best hot chocolate. He closed his eyes. Enjoyed her prattle.

"Montana is nicknamed Big Sky Country for its wide-open spaces," she said. "Hey, are you listening? I'm sharing important things here."

He inwardly smiled before looking out the windshield. "And I've heard every word. Where are we headed next?" It looked like they were leaving town.

"I thought I'd show you Miracle Lake. It's really pretty this time of year, and we could go ice skating if you want."

It took Theo a moment to answer. His mom had told him about the special place Miracle Lake held in her heart. He'd planned to visit it on his own and set in motion her wish, but right now felt good, too. "I'd like that. My mom skated there as a kid and fished there with my grandfather during the summers."

"Did she tell you the reason for its name?"

"She did. In fact, she had a miracle happen there."

Rowan glanced at him with surprise and a spark of curiosity in her eyes he'd come to take pleasure in. "Tell me."

"My grandfather never learned to swim, but loved being on the water. The first time he took my mom out to fish, she was six and while she knew how to swim, my grandfather told her she had to wear a life jacket. She agreed, but only if he wore one, too, something he didn't normally do. That day, the boat tipped and they both landed in the water. If my grandfather hadn't been wearing a life jacket, there was a good chance he would have drowned."

"Wow. I've heard about extraordinary things happening, going as far back as the 1890s, but no one remembers anything specific."

"Do you believe in miracles?" Theo asked.

She dug her teeth into her bottom lip and his body tightened in response, catching him off guard. "Yes."

"Me, too," he managed to say with a normal voice, his attention out the windshield. She continued to captivate him in ways that were getting harder and harder to pass over.

There were no other cars on the road as they took their first blind curve. Rowan's speed was on the conservative side, but she still didn't have time to avoid the garbage can rolling toward them in the middle of the lane. It must have fallen off the pickup truck Theo saw up ahead.

"Hold on!" She gripped the steering wheel with both hands and slammed on the brakes. The car skidded and despite her efforts, ran over the large rubber container. "Crap," Rowan said, the trashcan staying lodged underneath their car and grinding them to a halt as she white knuckled the vehicle over to the shoulder. They stopped with an uncomfortable jolt.

"Are you okay?" She reached out to put her hand on his chest. By her knit brows and pursed lips, he thought she might be checking to see that his heart was still beating.

"I'm fine. You?" He covered her hand with his.

"I'm good." She pulled her arm back. Jumped out of the car.

He met her at the hood, the smell of burned rubber immediately hitting his nose. They bent at the same time to look under the car and knocked foreheads. "Ow," they groaned at the same time.

Rubbing her temple with a half smile on her pretty face, she pointed to the snow behind him with her free hand and said, "You. Over there, out of harm's way."

"What are you planning on doing?"

"Seeing if I can pull this rubber road hazard out."

"I can help."

"No. You can't. Do you know how many vehicles are hit when they're stuck on the side of a road? Too many, and I refuse to have an international incident arise if you get hurt while with me."

Theo laughed. "International incident? I think you're giving me too much credit."

"Whatever. Please just go make a snow angel or something." She waved him away.

"No can do." He knelt to check out the damage under the car. "I don't know much about cars, but I think we're going to need some help here. We don't want to do damage to the undercarriage by trying to pull this out."

She huffed out a breath as she crouched down beside him. "Crap," she said again. "Okay, let me grab my phone and call roadside assistance, and then we'll both wait off the road."

That he could agree to. He kept an eye on her—and oncoming cars—as she retrieved her cell and flipped on the hazard lights. She had the phone to her ear walking back to his side.

"Do you want the good news or the bad news first?" she asked, tucking and zipping the phone into her jacket pocket while she ushered him into the snow. Her concern made the center of his chest warm.

"The bad news."

"It seems today is a busy day for our towing department, so it's going to be about an hour wait."

An hour stuck with Rowan was anything but bad. "And the good news?"

"My NASCAR driving skills somehow dislodged the top off the trash can and it's sitting right over there." She nodded over his shoulder.

Sure enough, the lid sat a couple of car lengths behind him. "That's good news because…?"

She eyed him like, *seriously?* But then said, "That's right. Snow is a foreign substance to you." She put her hands on his upper arms and turned him so his back was to her. "Tell me what you see."

They'd landed on a stretch of deserted road, so there was nothing but snow and trees. He told her as much.

"There's something else." Her breath feathered across the back of his neck, making him hot on this very cold winter afternoon.

When he didn't answer right away, she said, "A hill. Come on." She strode to the garbage can lid, picked it up, and trekked toward the giant slope perfect for sliding down.

Now he got it.

"Have you ever gone sledding before?" she asked.

His boots left deep prints while they slogged up the small hillside. "I haven't." He'd skied a few times in Switzerland but preferred activities in warmer weather.

"I'll go first then. I think if you watch me once, you'll have no trouble. Not that this is difficult or anything. You just sit and slide."

"I'm familiar with the concept," he said lightly. "But rather like the idea of watching you."

She turned her head down and away from him, a shy reaction he hadn't expected from someone so at ease with herself. He hoped she wasn't also bothered. Shit. He really didn't need to say everything he thought out loud.

"Be sure you don't put your legs out and try to stop with your feet," she said after a few moments of quiet. "I don't want you to twist your ankle again or anything."

"Noted." He thought about taking the rubber lid from her, for no other reason than to be a gentleman, but she'd probably get mad at him and tell him she was perfectly capable of holding the thing and walking at the same time.

They arrived at the top of the hill. While not very high, Theo still enjoyed the view. He lifted his face to the cloud-covered sky. Even devoid of the blue he was used to, he found its expanse breathtaking. The air fresh and pine scented.

"I like to go really fast so would you mind giving me a

push?" Rowan asked.

Theo twisted around to find her sitting cross-legged on the saucer. She was gathering her hair and tying the long strands into a knot. "I'd be happy to." He put his hands on her back. "Ready?"

"Ready."

The joy and excitement in her voice reminded him of when he was a boy and he and his brother rolled down grassy hills in the countryside. Otis would always wait for him to say "ready" before they took off like logs down the hill, racing to get to the bottom first, but laughing the entire way, too.

"Have fun," Theo whispered in Rowan's ear, his mouth just below her earlobe. Then he gave her a sturdy push.

"Woo hoo!" she yelled, flying down the hill, her hands gripping the lip of the garbage top. The saucer spun, taking her for a backward ride, and blessing him with a view of her gorgeous grin. She leaned back slightly, lifted one side of the rubber, and whirled back around. The girl knew the fine art of sledding.

She continued to fascinate him with her intelligence, liveliness, and desire for fun.

"That was so fun," she shouted from the bottom, as if she'd read his mind.

He couldn't pull his gaze off her as she made her way back to him. Her nose and cheeks were pink. Wisps of hair fell around her face. She carried herself with a grace he found appealing on so many levels, but mostly because she didn't take herself—or him—too seriously.

When she stood in front of him, slightly out of breath, it took all his strength not to wrap his arms around her waist, haul her close, and kiss the hell out of her.

"What?" she asked, narrowing her eyes in suspicion.

"Nothing." He took the offered trash lid, set it down. He couldn't fold himself onto it quite the same way Rowan did, but at the moment, all that mattered was getting some distance from her. Hands in the snow, he pushed himself off.

And had a blast "sledding" down a hill for the first time.

Time seemed to stand still after that as he and Rowan alternated turns down the slope, teasing each other about form and giving out scores of one to ten like it was an Olympic event.

She'd just gotten situated for another ride when a tow truck pulled up in front of her car. Had it been an hour already? Quickly, and without thinking, he sat down behind her, cradling her between his thighs and wrapping his arms around her waist. They both needed to get down the hill and this seemed like the best solution.

Her breath hitched, her body tensed.

"I thought we could do this last run as a team," he said quietly. "But if you'd rather—"

"It's okay." She relaxed against him. "This is good."

Having her in his lap felt better than good. Even with a bulky jacket on, she was soft. Her hair smelled like citrus shampoo. And she fit.

"Here we go." He shoved them off. They gathered speed quickly. Rowan's sounds of glee made him smile inside and out as the wind rushed their faces.

They started to slow, the slope evening out. Theo shifted slightly and the heel of his boot got stuck in the snow for a second. They spun out of control, pitched to the side, and crash landed. Their bodies tangled, rolled as one, and came to a stop with him on top of her.

Worried he was crushing her, he quickly pushed up onto his elbows. Her eyes were closed and her long, black lashes almost reached the tops of her pink cheeks. Snow clung to her hair. He gulped. She was beautiful. "Sorry about that. Are you okay?"

He was acutely aware of her chest rising and falling as she tortured him with silence for several seconds before finally opening her baby blues and saying, "That. Was. Epic." Then she broke into a fit of laughter.

And God, it made her even more beautiful. She wasn't irritated or flustered by their crash, but tickled by it. He stared down at her, enjoying her sound and the crinkles in the corners of her eyes. His body covered hers, making contact in so many good places, making him hungry for more. He hadn't meant to like Rowan as much as he did, but she was great, and every interaction elevated his attraction to her.

Any affection had to be buried, though. He had a life

waiting for him back home.

The thought bothered him more than he cared to admit.

How could it not when she stopped laughing and any pretense of this being a simple friendship vanished? The way she looked up at him, with desire and playfulness, was one hell of an aphrodisiac. He imagined she saw the same expression mirrored back at her.

He slid one hand in her hair to cradle the back of her head. With his other hand, he cupped her cheek. He'd never wanted to kiss someone so badly. At the moment, he didn't care about the consequences. If he didn't get to make her lips sore, suck her tongue into his mouth, and find out what she tasted like, he'd regret it.

"Rowan," he whispered.

She reached up and brushed the hair off his forehead. "Yes, Theo."

Was that a question or an answer? It sounded like an answer. A *yes, please kiss me before I lose my mind, too.* But he had to be sure. He didn't want to ruin the connection they'd already established.

"I want to—"

"Hey, Ro! You going to play in the snow all day or come tell me what happened?" a man shouted good-naturedly from behind them. The interruption had Rowan fisting the front of Theo's jacket and pushing him off her like he was breathing fire.

"On my way," she called back, jumping to her feet. She

brushed the snow off her jeans, then gave him a look of regret. Over being interrupted, or letting something almost happen between them, he didn't know. "We... That... I can't..."

He was at a loss for words as well.

"I'm going to head back to the car now." She motioned with her thumb over her shoulder and took off toward the road.

Theo watched her go, tied up in knots he had no idea how to let go of.

Chapter Seven

ROWAN COULDN'T STOP thinking about Theo almost kissing her. Their mouths had been mere inches from each other and his incredible blue eyes had gleamed with desire focused entirely on *her*. A small-town girl more tomboy than girly-girl and who had to be a million miles away from the women he usually gave attention to.

She leaned against the hospital wall and remembered his body heat, the feel of his hard angles against her soft ones. She'd never wanted a kiss as much as she'd wanted his. But it was wrong. Unprofessional. These feelings of longing and adoration were unacceptable and a sure way to lose more respect.

"Rowan?"

She startled at the sound of her name and turned her head to find the man from last night—Annabelle's father—checking out her mural. "Hi," she said.

"You finished it."

"Yes." She'd stayed all night to do so, too keyed up from her day with Theo to even think about sleep. In the quiet late night and early morning hours, the deserted hallway had been a refuge from unwanted thoughts. Completely lost in painting, she forgot all about the world outside. For a little while at least.

"It's going to be a big hit."

"I think so, too." She had a funny feeling in the pit of her stomach that made her think this mural *was* going to be well received. She'd never worked harder at something or cared more deeply. Relief washed over her.

He chuckled. "Good to know you don't lack confidence."

"I'm good at faking it, but my older brother did drill conviction into me. If I wanted to beat him at something, I had to go in thinking I could."

"How'd that work out?"

"If you ask him, he'll tell you he *let* me win, but I know better." She pushed away from the wall. "How's Annabelle?"

"She's doing better, thanks."

"I'm happy to hear that." Rowan peeked at his left hand. No wedding ring. Which didn't mean he wasn't married, but if he was, where was his wife? It was on the tip of her tongue to ask, but it wasn't her business. She just hoped he had someone to lean on while his daughter was hospitalized.

"Congratulations on a job well done," he said, moving down the hallway.

"Thanks and best wishes to your daughter."

Rowan watched him disappear around the corner. When she turned around, Bea stood beside her, the older woman's attention on the mural. "Hey, what are you doing sneaking up on me here?" Ro asked.

"A little birdy told me you decided to pull an all-nighter, and I wanted to be one of the first to see the finished product."

Bea knew about the mural? The only people Ro had told were her parents and Cassidy.

"I may be retired, but I've still got eyes and ears all over these hallways," Bea said. "Now c'mere so I can give you a congratulatory hug. It's spectacular."

Rowan stepped into Bea's open arms. "Why did you keep this magnificent mural a secret?" Bea asked.

"It's not like it was a total secret," Rowan said, releasing her hold on Bea. "I've just always been private with my artwork." She pictured her closet where several paintings were tucked behind her jeans.

"Your holiday cards beg to differ."

Bea had her there. "Those are small tokens of friendship. This is the biggest thing I've done and I didn't...I was a little nervous about it." She didn't want a lot of attention for this. Not this hobby that felt super personal. Her writer's voice was much different than her artist's brush stroke, and if she hadn't loved the way the mural turned out, she wanted to fail without spectators this time. Or pity.

She'd had enough of both the past few months.

"You know what I think?" Bea said.

"No, what do you think?"

"That we need some baked apple-cider donuts and coffee."

"I like the way you think." Ro stuck her elbow out and the two of them made their way to breakfast arm in arm. Bea was like a grandmother to Ro and sharing this time together meant a lot. "It was really sweet of you to come down here. Thank you."

Bea bumped Rowan's hip. "I love you like a granddaughter, you know."

"The love flows both ways," Ro said, bumping her back.

A little while later, after a short walk with the dogs (she promised them a longer one tomorrow), quick shower, and change into comfy warm clothes, Rowan sat in Bea's kitchen eating homemade apple-cider donuts and drinking her second cup of coffee. She needed the caffeine if she planned to stay awake for the rest of the day. She had a date with her laptop this afternoon to work on her story for the Courier.

"What's David up to this morning?" The retired engineer usually didn't stray far from Bea. He loved to dote on her.

"He and Theo went to do some Christmas shopping," she said happily.

"You guys are loving having him here, aren't you?"

"It's been wonderful. I'm going to miss him terribly when he goes home." Bea lifted her coffee cup, but paused before taking a sip. "He told me he asked you to be his date for the Ball."

"Yeah, I figure this is my only chance to be a prince's

plus one."

"Is that all it is?"

"*Have you seen him*?" Ro said flippantly. She hoped that diffused any notion that Bea might have about this being anything other than a superficial date. Bea chuckled. "Plus, someone needs to protect him from the single women of Marietta."

"Is that so?" Bea asked with a tilt of her head.

Rowan almost choked on her donut. Bea had stars in her eyes. Matchmaking stars. It wouldn't be the first time Bea had *suggested*—translation: fixed Rowan up—with a nice, single young man. A NSYM was not on Ro's to-do list.

Not that Theo fell into that category exactly.

"The two of you have been spending a lot of time together," she added.

"Yes, because of my story for the Courier. No other reason." No reasons she would voice out loud, anyway. Reasons like she found herself wanting to be around him all the time.

"Has he mentioned Elisabeth?"

"A little." *We're friends. Elisabeth and I, so I suppose that's something*, he said that night they'd danced.

A melancholy expression passed over Bea's kind face. "They don't know each other very well, and what they do know is purely on an acquaintance level. It makes me sad that he doesn't get to marry for love."

"They could grow to love each other," Ro offered. Her stomach jumped at the suggestion.

"I suppose, but I find it heartbreaking that I lost my daughter to Theo's father and yet the king doesn't want his son to experience that same kind of love affair." Bea took a shaky breath. "Theo deserves someone special. He's such a caring, loyal, exceptional young man."

Spoken like a true grandmother.

Rowan glanced at the clock on the wall. Almost eleven-thirty. "He is," Ro said, "and that won't change once he's married." She started to gather her plate and mug. "Thank you for breakfast."

"You're not leaving, are you?"

"I should. I've got a lot of writing to do today." She owed Emmaline an article for the pet column, too.

"Have one more donut," Bea insisted as she put another on Ro's plate.

"Hello!" David called out. "Sorry I'm late."

Bea quickly got to her feet. "Oh, shoot. I forgot David has a dentist appointment. No need for you to rush out, though."

Rowan studied Bea. The woman didn't forget anything. She also conveniently turned around to pick up her purse so Rowan couldn't consider her any further.

David and Theo strode into the room, lots of shopping bags in their hands. Surprise registered on both men's faces when they saw her. "Hi," she said.

"Morning," they answered together.

"We'd better hurry," Bea said, grabbing David's hand the

second he put his bags down. "We don't want to be late for your dental appointment. Theo, you'll keep Rowan company while she finishes her breakfast, won't you? There are plenty of apple-cider donuts left. You can tell me how you like them later." She hustled her husband out of the kitchen. "Rowan, sweetie, I'm proud of you."

"Goodbye," David shouted from out of eyesight.

Theo put his packages down and took a seat beside her at the kitchen table. He looked especially drool worthy in his maroon zip-neck pullover and beanie. "What just happened?"

"I believe this is your grandmother's attempt to get us alone."

"There's no dentist appointment?"

"Maybe?" Ro said with a slight shrug. "But she's a master at chess, so you know…"

He picked up a donut. "I did not know that." Took a bite. He made eating really fun to watch. "So on top of being sweet, kind, a great cook, and a good listener, she's got a shrewd side."

"Yes."

"And she likes the idea of the two of us being together."

Rowan wasn't sure if he meant together, together, or together to hang out since they were the same age and she was writing an article on him. She went with the latter to keep things from getting awkward. "She's one of my biggest supporters, but this time has a vested interest in my article for the Courier, so yes, she wants me to get to know you."

"I've enjoyed getting to know you in return." He picked up her coffee mug and took a sip.

Which left her with having to take a bite of her third donut since she needed a minute to think of what to say to that. She normally spewed comebacks without thought, but Theo short-circuited her brain or something.

And made her want to take a sip from the exact same spot his lips had been on. *This is not like never wanting to wash your hand after you shook Mark Wahlburg's when he was in town filming a movie.* That was ten years ago. She'd matured.

"Looks like you got a lot accomplished this morning." She nodded toward the shopping bags. "Does this mean you're excited about your first white Christmas?"

"I'm looking forward to spending it with Bea and David, yes." In past years, Bea and David had joined Rowan's family on Christmas Day since it was just the two of them.

"Here at the house?" she inquired, hoping this year would be different. Then feeling bad about it. She shouldn't hold tradition against Theo just because she found it harder and harder to be around him and not feel things.

"I'm assuming so." He popped the last bite of his donut into his mouth, chewed, and swallowed. "Do you know something I don't?"

"Nope." She didn't.

"How does your family spend the day?"

She cut the donut on her plate and gave half of it to Theo. "We start with—" She paused at the sound of his cell phone, interested to know who was calling him.

He pulled the phone out of his pocket, took a quick glance at the screen, and brought it to his ear. "Hello?… Hi, Elisabeth… Sure, hold on just a minute…" He moved the phone away from his mouth and stood. "I'm going to take this in the other room. Sit tight for a few?"

"Actually," she said, jumping to her feet, "I was on my way out before you got here, so you stay put and talk to Elisabeth. We can talk more later." She speed walked out of the kitchen without a look back. Right before she got to the front door, she overheard Theo speaking but couldn't decipher his exact words.

Once outside, she took a large gulp of fresh mountain air before jogging home. Back inside the comfort and safety of her four walls, she wiped the stupid moisture at the corner of her eyes.

From the cold. Not from anything else.

THEO DIDN'T LIKE how Rowan had taken off so abruptly. He should have just spoken to Elisabeth in the kitchen, but it was too late now.

Staring at the half a donut Rowan had kindly put on a napkin in front of him, he sat back down, suddenly unsure of everything. "Elisabeth, how are you?"

"I'm in love," she blurted out.

"With?" he asked calmly. She couldn't mean him.

"His name is James, and we've been seeing each other for a couple of months. He's everything I want Theo, and he loves me, too. When I told him about us, he begged me not to go through with it. I'm sorry if this upsets you, but what are we going to do? I like you, but I don't want to marry you."

A huge flood of relief rushed over him. Quickly followed by despair. He didn't want to marry Elisabeth either, but they had a duty to uphold. Their engagement wasn't about them so much as it was about the monarchy.

"It's ridiculous of our parents to think in this day and age that something like this is a good idea," she continued. "Please tell me you agree."

"I do agree. And I'm glad you've called to tell me how you feel. This isn't something I want, either, but I'm not sure we have a choice."

Elisabeth sighed through the phone. "You're too loyal."

"Is there such a thing?" He loved his father. Loved his country. He'd let his dad down once before and swore never to do it again. Doing the right thing took precedence over self-fulfillment.

This time.

Theo's decision years ago to get his pilot's license rather than dedicate himself to royal duties filled his thoughts. His father had been disappointed to the point that they didn't speak for months. The rift had deeply hurt Theo's mom, but finally his father had come around.

"At the sacrifice of our own happiness, yes," Elisabeth said.

Theo rubbed the back of his neck. "Listen, I can't do anything from here, so how about we meet when I get back?"

"When is that?" she asked, restlessness in her tone.

"The second."

"That's a little more than two weeks away. Can you cut your visit short and fly back sooner?"

"No." His time in Marietta had far exceeded his expectations and connecting with his grandparents was a gift he didn't want to end before necessary. They were amazing people and there were more stories to share, more holiday traditions and events to take part in. He also wanted more time with Rowan.

"There's something else I need to tell you then. There's a chance…"

"Yes?"

She expelled a deep breath. "That I might be pregnant. We haven't really been—"

"I don't need any details," he cut off, but he still sounded supportive. "When will you know?"

"Next week. I'm sorry."

This would change everything. And Theo wouldn't be held to blame. "No apology necessary. How do you feel about it, though? What does James say?"

"We'd both be thrilled."

"Then I will be, too." Either way, however, they couldn't marry. Not when she clearly wanted a life with another man. Theo refused to take that away from her. His father would have to understand. "Call me when you find out and we'll go from there."

"I will. Thanks, Theo."

"We'll figure this out. Don't worry, okay?"

"Okay. I'll talk to you soon."

They hung up, and Theo immediately called his brother. Otis answered after the first ring.

"Hello, little brother. I was wondering when I'd hear from you. How is small-town USA?"

The tightness in Theo's chest loosened at the sound of his brother's voice. "It's great. You're missing out."

"On snow? I don't think so."

"Say hi to Theo for me!" Miranda, Otis's wife, yelled in the background.

"Did you hear that?" Otis asked, knowing Theo had. They teased Miranda all the time about her loud—and lovely—voice. It was one of the first things that had attracted Otis to the princess.

"I did. Say hello back."

Otis relayed Theo's message, then said, "So tell me why you don't sound like things are great."

His brother always picked up on his moods with ease. "I just got off the phone with Elisabeth." He went on to tell

Otis about their conversation.

"This is good news."

"Yes and no." Yes because he didn't want to marry Elisabeth. No because he knew his father wouldn't like it. Elisabeth's family might let her off the hook, but the king wanted Theo married and finding another princess to fit the role wouldn't be difficult.

"It's time you stood up to Dad," Otis said, not for the first time. While close to their father, he also butted heads with him far more than Theo did. Which made it especially hard for Theo to think about doing the same now.

Theo also couldn't help think about the words his mom had whispered to him when she'd first been hospitalized. *If the bleeding is serious and I don't make it, take care of your father for me*. Certainly his mom hadn't meant for him to be miserable in the process.

"Maybe," Theo agreed. A certain woman with her hair piled on top of her head and perceptive blue eyes who shared donuts flashed through his mind. She unsettled every single part of him. He felt himself feeling something more for her. Something he craved to explore.

There was nothing holding him back now. Elisabeth had freed him from any loyalty tying him to her.

"No maybe's this time. If you don't, I will on your behalf."

"Not happening," Theo said firmly. "I'll handle this my way." His grieving father didn't need or deserve disobedience from his sons. Not when he believed he was doing the right thing.

"Fine. But you know where I stand. Now tell me about our grandparents."

Theo talked nonstop about the past couple of weeks. Without realizing it, he'd also included Rowan in much of his recollection.

"Sounds like you really like this reporter."

"I… She's different." In the best possible way. She didn't only stimulate his body. She fired up his mind.

The question was—what was he going to do about it?

Chapter Eight

"DO YOU LIVE in a castle? Ride a horse? Have a really big swimming pool with a slide? Can I see your crown?"

"Annabelle, slow down, sweetie. How about we give Prince Theodore a chance to answer one question at a time," Sean, the girl's father, said.

Theo smiled at the adorable six-year-old. She and her father had been in a terrible car accident, sideswiped by a sport utility vehicle. The impact had crushed Annabelle's side of the two-door sports car, leaving her with a broken leg, broken wrist, concussion, and internal bleeding. Thankfully, she was going to be fine. Sean had gotten away with nothing more than a sore neck and a pulled back muscle. Theo could see the anguish on the man's face—he'd give anything to change places with his daughter.

"No. No. Yes. I don't have it with me," Theo said.

She gave a little shrug. "Will you come talk at my school? Fridays are show and tell and no one has brought a prince before. Michaela brought a paylia…" She glanced at her dad.

"Paleontologist," Sean said.

"Yes, that, and everyone thought he was the best thing ever. Most of the time, we share things like toys and books and that gets kind of boring."

Theo chuckled. Annabelle was sweet and precocious. She'd probably get along fabulously with Rowan. *That was a weird thought.* "I'm honored that you think I rank up there with dinosaurs."

"Can you?" she pressed, her big brown eyes pleading. A line of stitches followed her hairline from her forehead to her ear. Today was Thursday. Did she mean tomorrow? If so, he'd be happy to, but he wasn't sure when she was being released.

"Any Friday that I'm here is yours."

Sean cleared his throat. "Unfortunately, we don't live here. We were just traveling through." There was more to the story of this father and daughter, but it wasn't Theo's place to ask.

He'd spent the last hour in the children's wing of the hospital to visit and give gifts from Santa. His shopping trip with David had proven quite the success, as all the kids loved the various toys Theo had purchased.

"Princes can go anywhere, though, right? Daddy will give you our phone number, and you could come see us when we get home."

The hope in Annabelle's voice tugged firmly on Theo's heart. He wished he could tell her yes. "I'm not sure my schedule would allow me to come see you, but I could send you something to share. Something from my country that no one else has."

Her little body shrank into the bed. "Okay, I guess."

She was killing him. "Have you ever had a pen pal? Someone you mail notes back and forth with?" he asked. She shook her head. "I haven't either. What do you say you be mine?"

"Really?"

"Really."

"That would be the bomb," she said excitedly, sitting taller and tossing a huge grin to her dad. "That's what Daddy and me say when something super great happens."

Theo took Annabelle's hand and kissed the back of it. "It's been a pleasure meeting you, Annabelle, and I look forward to your letters."

She giggled.

"What do you say, Belle?" Sean prompted.

"Thank you for the stuffed horsey." She brought the plush toy closer to her side. "I love him."

"You're welcome. Santa has given him strict instructions to help make you feel better."

"I do!"

With that, Theo took his leave, walking into the hallway with Sean. "Thank you, Your Highness. I haven't seen her this happy in a long time." The men shook hands.

Hawk stood at the nurse's station, being charming as ever by the look on the woman's face sitting at the desk. He enjoyed visits like this as much as Theo did and took up the slack with the staff when Theo lost track of time with the patients.

"It was my pleasure. Thank you for letting me visit with her. She's a great kid, and I hope she's out of here soon." He started toward the nurse's station. "Let me write down my mailing address for you."

"I'll be right back, Belle," Sean said over his shoulder.

They exchanged information, Theo said goodbye to the staff, and he and Hawk walked toward the elevators. Sean came along to grab something to eat from the cafeteria. As they turned a corner, color lit up the hall, and Theo took a closer look at the mural he'd passed by earlier.

"It's something, isn't it?" Sean said, nodding to the wall. "Annabelle claims she wants to be an artist now."

"We've visited a lot of hospitals and never seen anything like this," Hawk said, stopping to admire the whimsical painting. "I bet it cheers the shit out of the kids."

"It's definitely cheered up Annabelle. I wish I'd thought to have the artist visit with her before she finished."

"If she's local, she'll probably come back," Theo said. The people of Marietta were the nicest he'd ever met.

"You're right. Rowan seemed like the type of woman who definitely would."

"Rowan?" Theo and Hawk said at the same time.

"You know her?" Sean asked.

Theo and Hawk exchanged glances. Hawk raised his

eyebrows and a crooked smile pulled at his mouth. "Yes," Theo said, turning to *really* look at the mural. He took in every single detail, committing them to memory.

He had no idea how long he stood there, but it was long enough for Hawk and Sean to return with food in their hands.

"Yep," Hawk said, slapping Theo on the back. "My man is in deep."

"A friend of mine manages artists," Sean said. "I'll mention Rowan to him."

"You should ask Rowan about that first," Theo said, knowing instinctively she wouldn't want to be caught off guard. She'd said painting was personal. A hobby. Did she love writing as much as she clearly loved painting?

Her heart, her innate cheerfulness, was stamped across the wall for everyone to see. He'd bet she didn't realize that. And what a gift it was to others.

"All right. If I get the chance, I will. It was nice meeting you, and thanks again," Sean said on his way back to his daughter.

"Your girl is seriously talented," Hawk said once Sean was out of sight.

"She's not my girl." It was stupid to start something with her when he couldn't come close to finishing it. Despite the nagging feeling that Rowan might be the woman to steal his heart, he had to remember his place and where he belonged. And that was beside his father in Montanique.

Hawk took a bite of his apple and walked alongside Theo away from the mural. "You can keep telling yourself that or you can do something about it with the time we've got left here."

He hadn't seen or talked to Rowan since yesterday morning when he'd blown it with the phone call from Elisabeth. The ball was in two days. They had nothing planned until then, but a gesture to let her know he was thinking about her couldn't hurt.

"There's a larger town north of here, right?"

"Bozeman?" Hawk asked as they entered the elevator.

"That's it. Let's head there. I need to do some more shopping."

For his girl. Damn Hawk and his insinuation. Not that Rowan was the type to be anyone's without deciding it for herself first. His friend was right, though. With the time they had left, he wanted to be with Rowan in every way possible.

He'd always done the right thing, put others before himself—he and Rowan had that in common—but it was their turn this time.

AT THE SOUND of the doorbell, Rowan couldn't answer it fast enough. Cassidy had called from the airport to say she and Nick were here and she'd be over to spend the night soon. Ro needed a girls' night with her BFF like flakes needed snow.

And wine needed grapes.

And Tootsie Roll Pops needed tootsie rolls.

"You're—" She stalled on the "here" as she opened the front door to find a deliveryman holding two large dress boxes. "Not Cassidy," she finished.

"Rowan Palotay?"

"Yes."

"Great. Mind if I put these down?"

"Oh, sorry. Please." She motioned for him to place them inside. Snow clung to the shoulders of his wool coat and his dark hair.

"There's two more," he said. "I'll be right back."

Who in the world was sending dresses to her? She hadn't told anyone she'd yet to get a gown for the ball, but someone obviously knew her well enough to know she'd waited until the last minute. What they didn't know was she hated to receive gifts like this.

Theo. Her heart gave a little sigh at the thought that he might be responsible. Maybe she didn't mind being on the receiving end this time.

The delivery guy returned—with her best friend right behind him. "Looks like I got here just in time."

"Hey!" Rowan said, hugging Cassidy in hello. "You mean these aren't from you?" she joked.

"Sign here, please," the delivery guy said, handing her a clipboard. She signed, said thanks, and shut the door. The tower of dress boxes reached past her waist. It was a little surreal and a little exciting, and she was almost afraid to look inside them.

"Open the card," Cass suggested impatiently as she dropped an overnight bag by the coffee table.

Rowan slid the white card stock out of the gold envelope with slightly shaking hands. She held the note in front of her so Cass could read it at the same time.

Dear Rowan,

I pictured you in each of these dresses and hope you find one of them your type…because you're mine and you'll look beautiful in all of them.

See you Saturday,
Theo

"Oh my God. That is so romantic! He really likes you, Ro. You're his type. Which coming from a prince is pretty freaking awesome."

Rowan read the note again. And again. He'd handwritten it. Knew exactly what he was saying. Why do this now? Was it about more than just the ball?

"Say something," Cassidy said. "I've known you for twenty-five years and you've never been this quiet."

"We need to send them back." She stuffed the card back in the envelope and placed it atop the box. "This is unprofessional, and I can't accept them. What made him think any part of this was okay?" She plopped down on the couch, her gaze unfocused, her breathing shallow.

"Ro," Cass said softly, sitting and linking their arms. "What's going on?"

"He's engaged. Well, almost. But still." She went on to explain Theo's situation in painstaking detail, hoping it would make her feel better. It didn't.

"Do you think he wants to have a fling with you?"

She thought about that. They had chemistry ten times over, but... "He doesn't strike me as a fling kind of guy. Besides, I'm writing a story on him. That means no flinging or I'm flung from my job. If Emmaline thinks I'm acting in any way but professional, she'll fire me. I'm trying to restore my reputation, not damage it further."

"This is an entirely different situation than before. Your integrity is intact, Ro."

"Is it?" If Cassidy knew the things going on in Ro's head, the dirty things she wanted to do with Theo, Cass wouldn't be so quick to say that.

"Yes," Cassidy said adamantly. "This is all on the prince, not you. You didn't ask him to buy you a dress, did you?"

"No."

"Lead him on?"

"No." At least she didn't think she had. Yes, they'd teased the line of professionalism. They flirted, almost kissed, and had intense eye contact, but she hadn't blatantly led him to believe their mostly innocent exchanges meant more.

"Tell him you wanted to see him naked?"

"No!" But she did. So, so badly.

"I don't see the problem then. You are his date. People are going to see the two of you together."

Ro turned her head to study her best friend. "I feel like we've role reversed. Since when are you the one telling me how it is?"

"What can I say? Your brother's been a good influence on me." She nudged Ro with her shoulder. "Besides, you deserve some fun with a hot guy."

Fun. That's all this thing with Theo was. He had a pre-arranged fiancée waiting for him back home. Royal duties and commitments. This month was a vacation from his real life. A chance to bond with grandparents he'd never met and learn about where his mom grew up.

And being a prince, of course he was smooth and charming and enjoyed making a girl feel appreciated. Yes, once again, that's all this was. Appreciation.

She eyed the gift boxes. She *was* curious to see what type of dress Theo wanted to see her in. Plus, she *did* need something to wear.

"One of those dresses also means we don't have to go shopping for one tomorrow."

Rowan sprang to her feet. She hated clothes shopping. "It's on like Donkey Kong." She pulled the box from the top of the pile to the side, lifted the lid, and peeled back the tissue paper. A black gown sat inside. She swallowed a knot of emotion as she took the dress out, arms raised above her head so they could see the length of it.

"That. Is. Gorgeous," Cass said. "Hurry up and try it on."

It fit like a glove, the bodice tight, but not uncomfortable. The pleated, off-the shoulder neckline and banded short sleeves were elegant and classic. Halfway down, the skirt flared out and the hem fell to the floor with a train at back. A freaking train!

"Wow," Cass said.

Ro did a little twirl, unable to stop herself from smiling. Holding the extra-long material in her hand, she spun all the way to the kitchen where she and Cass decided a peppermint Schnapps shot had to be tossed back in between dresses.

The next gown looked straight out of a fashion magazine. Champagne colored with a floral-embroidered applique, Ro had never seen anything so pretty. It was strapless with a fitted bodice, but had a full skirt that draped at the side.

"Don't move," Cassidy ordered. "We need pictures." She pulled her phone out of her bag. "I wish I had my camera."

"I thought professional photographers never left home without it."

"They don't. It's in my other bag with Nick."

"Photos really aren't necessary." Ro started down the narrow hallway to her bedroom so she could see herself in the bathroom mirror.

"Oh, yes they are. Look over your shoulder at me."

Only because Cass was her best friend did Ro oblige. A few more pictures and a long stare in the mirror and they were back in the kitchen.

"You're enjoying this," Cass said as she poured them each a shot.

"Yes," Ro admitted. She'd never gone into her mom's closest as a kid to play dress up, too busy trying to keep up with her brother and whatever he was doing. Letting her femininity show tonight was fun.

"I'm glad. You deserve this."

"Cheers!" They clinked shot glasses then giggled all the way back to the living room.

"Okay, this has got to be said. The prince has definitely been studying your body," Cass announced as dress number three, a long-sleeve topaz lace gown with sapphire blue lining comfortably hugged Ro's curves. Rhinestones decorated the round neckline.

Ro glanced behind her at the slight train before lifting the material and floating to her bathroom for a better look in the mirror. If Theo's goal was to make her feel like her feet weren't touching the ground, he'd succeeded.

"Say bee's knees!" Cassidy snapped a picture, then another hundred thousand. Shots of peppermint Schnapps hit the back of their throats next.

They rather clumsily returned to the living room, Ro tripping over the hem of the dress before righting herself with a hand on the last dress box. She swept her free hand across her forehead as Cass tugged down the back zipper. "Is the room spinning?" Ro asked.

"You think so, too?"

They burst into a fit of laughter. "I'm so schnappy right now," Ro said, tossing the lid off the box. She'd been happier these past weeks with Theo than she'd been in a long time.

She slipped the last dress—a red one—on. From the front, the long-sleeve gown was simple and elegant: scalloped neckline, lace bodice, sheer long sleeves, banded waist, and a chiffon skirt with a floor-sweeping hem. But when Ro turned, her best friend whistled.

"Holy Beyoncé J-Lo, that is sexy. Look." Cass held her phone up in camera mode so Ro could see the open triangle back that dipped dangerously low. "By the way, boy short panties under any of these dresses are a no-no. You have to wear something lacy and tiny."

Rowan ran her hands down the soft fabric She felt sexy. "No one is going to see what I have on underneath." Even though she very much wanted a certain someone to.

"Doesn't matter. You'll know."

Yeah, and be thinking about Theo sliding his fingers underneath the lace. Grazing her in just the right spot while his eyes melted into hers. She shivered.

It didn't matter what panties she wore, one touch from Theo to her arm or lower back and she'd feel it between her thighs the entire night.

"Kitchen," she said in lieu of further underwear talk,

where they Schnapped it up one more time. "Which one do you like best?" She loved all four of them.

"I think we should sleep on them."

"They'll wrinkle."

Cass waved her arm in the air. "No, no. I meant sleeponit."

"Slip knot it? What does that mean?"

They stared, no—concentrated, on one another before they cracked up. For the rest of the night they laughed, ate, watched television, paged through the bridal magazines Cass had brought with her, and added some peppermint Schnapps to their hot chocolates. When they fell into bed at midnight, Rowan pictured each of the four dresses hanging in different places in her house and slept with a smile.

Early the next morning, though, she woke with a headache the size of Yellowstone National Park. "Not so schnappy now, are you?" she mumbled, tiptoeing out of her bedroom so she didn't wake up Cassidy. Her four-legged crew expected her in less than an hour.

She padded into the kitchen to make coffee, her morning immediately brightening when she saw the black gown hanging from the curtain rod by the table. Four gorgeous gowns, each one making her feel like a princess. Tomorrow night, maybe she'd pretend she was one.

Coffee in hand a few minutes later, she sat down at her small desk to write Theo a thank-you note.

Dear Theo,

Okay, good start. She inwardly rolled her eyes. For a supposed writer, she didn't have a clue what to write next. A plain old thank you seemed inadequate. She dropped her head and noticed she'd slipped on her *Dear Santa* T-shirt to sleep in last night. Given Theo's high opinion of her banana tee, an idea took shape in her mind. She hoped he liked it.

Chapter Nine

ROWAN TIPTOED INTO the large foyer of the Bramble House Inn, hoping she'd go undetected, but Portia Bishop caught sight of her from across the room. Portia lived in the apartment above the garage and was Eliza's cousin's daughter. Rowan had only met her once at the chocolate shop where Portia worked, but when her friendly eyes met Ro's and Rowan pressed a finger to her mouth in a gesture of secrecy, Portia nodded and continued on her way.

The coast clear, Ro resumed her soft steps. She put the thank-you note she'd made for Theo on the bottom step of the curved staircase, then went right back to carefully walking on the balls of her feet. As she reached the front door, she let out the breath she'd been holding.

"Sneaking away without a hello?"

Dang it. She'd swear she'd been quiet as a mouse. Spinning around, her pulse hammered as she laid eyes on her prince. *The* prince, she meant. He wasn't hers. Not like that.

"Morning," she said while silently cursing her timing. "I was just leaving you a note." She nodded toward the stairs.

He turned and picked up the envelope. "Where's the

gang?" he asked, his attention on the card.

She had no idea what he was talking about. At her silence he lifted his head. "Oliver, Twist, Pepper...don't tell me...Sundance and...Buddy." The concentration on his handsome face morphed into a smile, his appeal unfair on both counts.

"I didn't see Pepper this morning, but the rest of the gang enjoyed our walk already. I stopped by here after I dropped them off."

He moved toward her and the closer he got, the more her neck and fingers tingled. There was something about the quiet in the room, the smell of pine and gingerbread in the air, and the thoughtful intensity on Theo's face. With no one else around, dressed in ordinary clothes, on an ordinary Friday morning, whatever this was between them felt important in a way she didn't want to examine too closely.

"I was at the hospital yesterday," he said, near enough to touch, "and saw your mural."

"You were? You did? Is everything okay?"

"Everything is fine. I was visiting the children's wing on behalf of Santa." His light tone indicated he'd made trips to lots of hospitals over the years. That he'd seen her mural made her want to hide, but she had to get used to people noticing it.

"The two of you are close?"

"Very. In fact, I'm the only one he lets take a peek at his naughty and nice list."

No way he said that. "Funny you should say that. Open your card." She dropped her gaze to his strong, capable-looking hands.

He lifted the flap of the envelope and pulled out the card. She hadn't wanted to be with him when he opened it, but now that she was stuck, she ignored the prick of unease between her shoulder blades.

A slow, heart-stopping grin took over his face as he read the card. She'd taken a selfie in her *Dear Santa* T-shirt earlier. The shirt said:

Dear Santa,
I have been good…
( ) most of the time.
( ) some of the time.
( ) once in a while.
(X) forget it—I will buy my own stuff.

Then she'd downloaded it to her computer, printed it, and handwritten, *Dear Theo, Thank you for making me feel good. I love the gowns. Fondly, Rowan.*

"I'm fond of you, too," he said, his voice a little deeper, his blue gaze boring into hers. "And I have to say, T-shirts are a good look on you. Have any more with sayings on them?"

"Maybe."

"I hope I get to find out."

Oh, boy. He inched closer. She inched back. "You are

good, Rowan, for so many reasons, but the most recent is the mural. It's spectacular."

"Thank you." She had no more room to maneuver, her butt hitting the wood front door, Theo filling the space in front of her.

He brushed her hair over her shoulder. "You're welcome."

She reached behind her for the door handle. "I should probably get going." No should about it. She needed to escape before she said or did something she couldn't take back. Or he did.

"Okay."

"Are you busy tonight?" She'd promised to play tour guide and despite her personal feelings, vowed to keep her word on that.

"I don't think so."

"My family is going on a sleigh ride. It's a Palotay tradition. Would you like to join us?" With her family around, there was no worry she'd act inappropriately. "Bea and David are welcome, too. And Hawk." The more the merrier. Just in case the fresh air and stars in the sky made her want to misbehave.

"That sounds great."

"Good. See you later, then." She opened the door and slipped through the narrow opening before Theo's magnetic pull kept her in place.

He'd seemed different this morning, but she couldn't put

her finger on what exactly had changed. She'd seen him serious and silly, concerned and carefree. And his royal upbringing appeared to be intruding less and less on "Marietta Theo." She imagined the same couldn't be said for all royals.

Walking away from the inn, she realized *that* was what had changed. In his jeans and flannel shirt, he'd looked more country than city, and at total ease with it.

At least for now, because in two weeks, he'd be back home to live the life he was born to lead.

MIRACLE LAKE WASN'T large like Theo had imagined it, but the snow-covered landscape in the middle of the woods where bright stars filled the night sky, made him feel like he'd stepped into a place larger than life. A "winter wonderland" his mom would say during her recollections of Christmas as a kid. He now understood what she meant.

He'd like to think she was looking down on him tonight, happy he'd chosen to spend the holiday in her hometown.

"Excuse me, Your Highness? Could we get a picture with you?"

Theo noticed Rowan sneak a glance at him before he gave his full attention to the group of girls wearing university knit hats who had exited the sleigh. "Sure," he said to the group leader.

The young women surrounded him amid thanks and

smiles while a bystander stood ready to snap the picture.

"He's not only handsome, but also gracious," Theo overheard Rowan's mom, Shari, say. She and her husband, Dennis, Rowan, Rowan's brother Nick, his fiancée, Cassidy, and Theo's grandparents all stood in line for the next sleigh ride. Hawk had begged off, worried his precious bum would be too cold.

Theo was always happy to pose for pictures. His mom had taught him to look kindly on everyone who sought him out. He grinned for the camera.

"Could we do a funny one, too?" one of the girls asked.

"That's my specialty," Theo said, much to the delight of his fans.

Everyone's stance changed and he wasn't sure about the girls, but he put his best funny face forward. The flash went off.

"Thank you so much!" the girls chimed in unison. A couple of them bounced up and down.

"My pleasure."

He turned back to his party to find them sitting in the waiting sleigh. Everyone but Rowan, that is. She stood beside the sleigh with a scowl on her face.

"It's only logical for you to ride with Theo," her mother was saying.

"Bea, wouldn't you like to take the ride with your grandson?" Rowan asked.

"Oh no, sweetie. I haven't done this with David in a long

time, and I'm good right here."

Theo was about to ask what the problem was when he figured it out. The sleigh was full. They must have miscalculated the number of available seats when climbing aboard. Although from the expression on his grandmother's face, this may have been another calculated move. He glanced at Rowan's mom and found the same sorry-not-sorry face.

He put his hand on Rowan's lower back to guide her a few steps back from the sleigh. "Looks like we're on the next one."

"That is the next one," she said. "There's only one sleigh."

"No, there isn't," her mother called out, a note to her tone that indicated Rowan knew that. "There's one more, and it looks available."

As if on cue, a handcrafted two-person horse drawn sleigh pulled up. Theo could kiss Rowan's mom and his grandmother for their planning. He wanted nothing more than to be alone with Rowan.

"Have fun! We'll meet up with you at the bonfire," Shari said, waving her hand as their sleigh started to move.

From his seat beside his mom, Nick shot Theo a warning glance. *Don't even think about touching my little sister.*

Theo ignored the look and waved goodbye. Rowan grumbled and marched over to the other sleigh. "I thought you liked my company," he said into her ear, not at all dismayed with her griping. He pretty much found everything she did appealing.

"That's the problem."

God, he loved that she didn't disguise her feelings. Especially since no other woman dared to show any side of her personality that wasn't in good spirits. Rowan might try to come off always in control, but when it was just the two of them, her guard wasn't foolproof. He reminded himself not to take that gift lightly.

They got comfortable in the sleigh, their bodies only inches from one another. Their driver went over some general information, then handed them a blanket. Rowan covered their laps with it. The horse began to trot and the jingling of sleigh bells played.

Theo planned to take advantage of every minute of their hour-long ride. He put his arm around her shoulders and gave a small tug, encouraging her to move closer. She looked over at him, her big blue eyes all the shades of the sea under the full moon, and he thought he'd never find another pair more beautiful.

He didn't know what she saw in his eyes, but he was grateful when she scooted over until they touched from shoulder to knee. Even with several layers of clothing between them, the contact had him growing—literally— uncomfortable behind the zipper of his jeans.

For the first several minutes, they relaxed quietly along the lakeside trail, winding through snow-covered pine trees underneath a sky populated with hundreds of twinkling stars.

"Best Christmas present," she said, breaking into the pleasant silence.

"You first."

"An easel and paints. I was ten and my mom also signed me up for one of those art schools that had tricks for teaching you how to draw. We used charcoals and paints and I loved it. It was easy for me and something my brother couldn't do very well. I was allowed to bring a guest once, and he came with me. His picture was awful, but I told him it looked great."

"I bet you were the best one in class."

She shrugged.

"Best for me was a puppy. My brother got a kitten the same year. They ended up great friends. But the best thing was I named her Otis."

"You named a female dog Otis?"

"Yes."

"Because…"

"Otis is my brother's name. I was five at the time and my mom suggested I name her after something that was important to me. My older brother was the most important thing in my life, so I named her after him."

Rowan laid her head on his shoulder. "That is so sweet. What did your brother think?"

"He thought it a terrible idea. I didn't like him mad at me and was going to change it, but then he purposely ruined the model airplane I'd worked weeks on with our dad so I made her middle name Otis, too. Otis Otis Chenery."

Rowan laughed. "I bet you were the cutest five-year old ever. What did Otis name his cat?"

"Yoda. The cat looked just like him."

"What's your middle name?"

With his free hand, Theo turned up the collar on his jacket to stave off the chill at his neck. "David."

She lifted her chin to look up at him. No words needed to be said. His mom had made sure to give each of her son's a piece of their grandfather. Otis shared their grandfather's middle name.

Before he wanted her to, before he had a chance to claim her mouth like he desperately craved to, she dropped her head. "What's yours?" he asked.

"Alexandra."

"Pretty."

"Thanks. Okay, worst Christmas present." She burrowed into him, like maybe she was cold, so he tightened the blanket around them.

"Easy. A doll," he said distastefully. He felt Rowan smile against him. "My brother got one, too. We were certain Santa had made a mistake and given the remote control cars we asked for to sisters on accident."

"Your parents tried to go outside stereotype and failed, uh?"

"Oh, yeah. Otis and I were positive if we left the dolls for

Santa to pick up, he'd exchange them for us. When they were still under the Christmas tree the following morning, we knew we were stuck."

"Did you play with them?"

"That would be a negative. We gave them away."

"So if you have a son one day and your wife wants to give him a doll to teach him the importance of not being typecast, you'd be against it?"

"Not at all."

"Good answer. Thing you're most afraid of."

"Promise not to laugh?"

"I promise."

He couldn't believe he was about to admit this to her, but she had a way of getting him to talk. With her, he couldn't stop the feelings in his chest, his muscles, and his head, that said he was safe with her. That she had no ulterior motives and genuinely liked his company. Despite her chagrin.

"Worms."

"You mean those tiny, extremely slow-moving creatures that live in the dirt?" That she spoke with unhidden drollness made him smile. "Yeah, they are totally badass and scary."

He bumped her leg with his. "I can explain."

"I sure hope so," she teased. "I mean, you put my fear of squirrels to shame."

"Squirrels?" he said, one side of his mouth quirking up.

"Do you know how mean they are?" she asked firmly.

"Very. There was an incident when I was a kid that I prefer not to talk about, so don't ask."

"You want to hear my story, though? Seems a little unfair."

"How about I promise to keep it between us?"

"All right." He would have told her anyway. "When I was seven, Otis put the longest worm on the planet in my spaghetti. He hid it under some other noodles so it wasn't obvious, and when I saw it move, I thought it was just a noodle at first, but then it lifted its head and I fell back in my chair, terrified. I've been bothered by them ever since."

"Exactly how long is the longest worm on the planet?"

"Really damn long."

She chuckled.

"Most embarrassing moment?" Theo asked, very much enjoying this latest question-and-answer session with Rowan. The sleigh glided over the snow with ease, their trail smooth, and he could listen to her talk all night. In the distance, he noticed a glow—the bonfire where they'd stop to have hot chocolate and holiday cookies before making the return trip.

"I don't really embarrass."

"What do you really do?"

She didn't answer right away. He tilted his head so his lips found her temple. He pressed them there, just under her fleece cap. "You can trust me not to judge you, Rowan. Nothing you say could make me like you any less."

"I make mistakes," she quietly revealed.

"We all do."

"Next question."

"Can I kiss you?"

She jerked away from him, turned her body to face his. "How can you ask me that?"

He smiled. "Is that a trick question?" God, she was beautiful when she got fired up. Challenged him.

His gaze was drawn to her pursed lips. "Do not look at my mouth," she said.

"Where should I look?"

"Over my shoulder somewhere," she said like he should have known that. "This ride is about the scenery. Not about anything else. I'm your reporter."

It stung to think all her questions were strictly professional, but she had made it clear from the start that everything between them was on the record. Which meant he had no idea where the line was. Not that it mattered. He liked Rowan. A lot. He suspected she liked him in return.

"I know that," he said evenly.

"So you understand my dilemma?"

Ah, she had a dilemma. Her admission stoked the desire thrumming through him like a lit fuse about to detonate. "I do, but I don't believe a newspaper article is a good enough reason not to explore the attraction between us."

"What about Elisabeth?" she asked, outraged on the princess's behalf. "I think that should be reason enough, Your Highness."

"Your protectiveness for someone you don't even know is insanely hot," he said. If he didn't think Rowan exceptional before, he would have now. "She's in love with someone else."

"*What?*"

"She called to tell me she was in love with her boyfriend, that they may be pregnant, and that she couldn't go through with the engagement."

"I don't know what to say."

"You could answer my question." Because, God help him, he was *this close* to kissing her with or without her reply.

"Where does this leave you?"

He should have known she'd fire back another question. A question he'd answer as truthfully as possible. "I'm not sure, but definitely without Elisabeth. I want her to be happy. Most likely my father will pick someone else who meets his requirements."

"So right now…" She drew in a slow breath.

"I'm free to do as I please." *Please let me do you.* He tried not to look at her with too much obvious preoccupation, but it wasn't easy.

She blinked slowly. Bit her bottom lip. Every time she did that, his body tightened. He understood her hesitancy. They were on borrowed time. Nothing could come from this instant, but powerful connection between them. Yet, it didn't hinder his desire for her. If it hampered hers, however, he'd respect her refusal and back off.

"Theo…" The sexy, breathy sound of his name made him reach out to cup the nape of her neck. She leaned closer. Her hand landed on his thigh underneath the blanket.

They didn't take their eyes off each other. They could have been in the middle of the North Pole for all Theo cared. The only thing that mattered to him was Rowan and kissing her so she knew what he felt wasn't fleeting. No confusion. No doubt. He cared about her, admired her, and wanted to show her how much for the rest of the month.

He brought her face to his, their cold noses touching. Her eyelids drifted shut.

And then she pressed her palm to his chest and lifted her head away. "I'm not," she whispered. "Free to do as I please."

"Is this about the newspaper?" he asked respectfully. He understood she wrote a pet column and that perhaps this was her first big interview, but they were two consenting adults.

"Yes."

"What if we finished the interview tonight and you had everything you needed to write the story by the time we reached the bonfire?"

"You really want to kiss me," she said playfully.

"You really want to kiss me, too."

She shook her head. "You're incorrigible."

He laced their gloved fingers together. "Is that a yes?"

"Has anyone ever told you no?" She measured him, her gaze drifting over his forehead, his cheeks, and the stubble on his jaw before lingering on his mouth.

"I'm not sure there's a right answer to that question. I can tell you I won't ever say no to you." Where that declaration came from, he had no idea.

She glanced away nervously before resuming eye contact. "You shouldn't say things like that. I could ask you to eat a worm."

He laughed. "Gummy, right?"

"Good comeback."

Theo fought the urge to pull her onto his lap and continue this conversation with her straddling him. The feeling of wanting her body atop his, even with their winter gear on, showed no signs of wavering.

All too soon, the sleigh came a stop. Damn it. They were at the bonfire. Her rueful expression gave him hope for later, though. And when she leaned forward and whispered, "Ask me again tomorrow night," his desire to take things further turned into a done deal.

Chapter Ten

ROWAN CLOSED HER laptop and let out a deep breath. Working on the article to set her career back on track was not all it was cracked up to be. She'd spent all day writing, finding it harder than she anticipated. Not because she didn't have enough material on Theo or didn't know the slant she wanted to use. It was hard because her subject kept intruding on her thoughts in ways only romance writers could write about.

His stupid blue eyes and sexy stubble and lips she couldn't stop fantasizing about were very inconvenient. Last night's sleigh ride had been romantic. Fun. A memory she'd hold tight to for a long time to come.

She drummed her fingers on her desk and contemplated tweaking one more thing on the story. *No.* She'd *finally* finished it. Sent an email to Emmaline letting her know it was done and would be in her inbox on Monday. Tomorrow, she'd give it one more read-through. If she peeked again now, she'd end up reading the whole thing.

She glanced at the clock on the wall. Crap. Bea and David were picking her up in an hour to drive to the ball. She put a hand on top of her head. Yep. Still in a messy, un-washed bun. Not that she planned to do anything special with her hair. Just shampoo, condition, blow-dry, curl, and maybe style in an up-do or twist with tendrils. She jumped to her feet, and yikes, a million pretzel crumbs fell from her lap onto the floor.

Clean up would have to wait, though, since she also had to shave her legs, exfoliate, file her nails, put clear nail polish on them, tweeze her eyebrows, and slap on some teeth whitening strips.

What?

She got her ass in gear, ignoring the nervous flutters in her stomach as she hurried into the shower like a girl getting ready to go on her first date and have her first kiss. Her nerves hadn't been close to this fluttery back then, or any other time, really. Rowan refused to examine what that meant. Although it could easily be attributed to Theo being a freaking prince!

Yes, that was it. It wasn't because the thought of having his mouth and hands on her put her entire being into a tailspin. And it wasn't because she wanted to tell him she was falling for him, that she'd never feel this way about anyone else again. Because that was ridiculous to the tenth power.

There was no scenario where things between them pro-gressed beyond the next two weeks, so she needed to chill and tell her heart to tone down the beats.

She accomplished everything on her beauty to-do list

with one minute to spare. When the doorbell rang, she was right there, pulling her long, black wool coat off the hanger.

"Rowan, you look gorgeous," Bea said, stepping inside. Outside, snow fell in light drifts, like the small florets of a dandelion when a person blows on the flowering plant to make a wish.

"Thank you." Bea wore a turquoise gown underneath her coat, and Rowan noticed it brought out the blue in her eyes.

"My grandson is going to swallow his tongue when he sees you," she added, peering around Ro to see the back of the dress.

"Bea. He is not. This isn't a real date. We're friends." She slipped one arm, then the other, into her coat.

"Don't kid yourself, sweetie. It's real."

It's not. If Rowan let it be real she was in danger of losing her heart. She'd yet to do that; worried she'd lose the biggest piece of herself to the wrong person. Besides, growing up with an older, protective brother, most local guys thought of her as a pal, not girlfriend material. In college she'd gone a little boy crazy, bouncing from boyfriend to boyfriend, but always keeping the upper hand and having a great time.

Cassidy had once told her she gave off a fun-loving, sometimes oblivious vibe. Meaning Rowan wasn't preoccupied with getting too serious with anyone, even if he wanted to get serious with her. Ro agreed. She knew when she met the *right* guy she'd give him all her pieces every minute of every day.

"Shall we?" Rowans asked, finished with the last button on her coat.

Once inside the car, David greeted Ro and the three of them made small talk on the way to the Graff Hotel. Snow continued to gently fall, bright festive holiday lights lit up homes and storefronts. Ro slouched in the back seat and stared out her window with a mixture of excitement and trepidation. The jitters pissed her off. She pressed her palms into the seat and straightened. Fear could be beaten with an attitude adjustment.

Theo is just a person. Albeit sexier than any man had a right to be. But tonight, family and friends would be in attendance, too. She'd mingle, eat, drink, and keep herself occupied so she didn't have time to dwell on the prince. By the time the hotel came into view, she was ready.

The lobby of the Graff Hotel always stole Rowan's breath for a second, but especially at Christmas time. The marble floor shimmered, wreaths hung in each towering oval window, and red velvet-wrapped greenery was swathed around the majestic columns and across archways. Gorgeous light fixtures bathed the large entrance in a golden rainbow of illumination. But the most spectacular feature was the giant fir Christmas tree decorated with sparkling white lights, twinkling glass ornaments, and velvet ribbons.

She, Bea, and David dropped their coats off at the coat check, then proceeded toward the Grand Ballroom. "I've got to make a quick stop at the ladies room," Rowan said. "I'll see you two inside."

After double-checking to make sure the lip gloss she'd put on in the car was actually on her lips and not around her mouth, too, she handed over her ticket at the ballroom door and stepped inside. The Daughters of Montana had really outdone themselves. Silver and red helium balloons covered the ceiling, adding a lustrous glow alongside the hanging crystal chandeliers. The tables were elegantly decorated with poinsettia centerpieces, china and crystal, and wow. Rowan looked a little more closely to find the white napkins were folded like swans. That must have taken forever to do.

Voices and laughter filled the room, and no one paid Rowan any attention as she looked around for a familiar face before moving further into the party. That was a lie. She really was searching for one person in particular. And she found him a split second later.

Good Lord, he looked amazing in a black tuxedo and white dress shirt open at the neck. No tie. That little fashion statement sparked warmth low in her belly and made her throb between her legs. *I'm in big trouble.*

Several people surrounded him in conversation, but pretty much everyone else in the ballroom had at least one eye on him. To Theo's left was Peta Dixon in a gorgeous red dress, and was that her ranch foreman, Hal, with her? Hmm. Next to them stood flirtatious Maddie Cash in a sparkly dress, Maddie's stepsister, Cynthia, and Cynthia's boyfriend Chad. To Theo's right were Brock and Troy Sheenan and their wives Harley and Taylor.

Theo would no doubt be the center of attention all evening, given the large number of guests with the opportunity to chat him up.

Having everyone's interest bothered her a little, even though it shouldn't. She had no claim to him. Thankfully, they'd prearranged to sit at the same table with their families for dinner so she'd get *some* time with him.

She should at least go say hello so he knew she'd arrived. He had, after all, asked her to be here. The women standing around him laughed at something he said, then his gaze slid to hers. She gave him a smile. He said something to his companions. They nodded and watched him walk across the dance floor toward her. His warm, extraordinary eyes were zeroed in on hers like he'd been waiting forever for her. Her feet took that to mean it was time to move toward him, too.

That silly saying, time stood still? It was a real thing. Happening to her right this minute. Her heart pounded in her chest as she and Theo erased the distance between them. Everyone except for the devastatingly handsome man in front of her faded into the background. And while she was vaguely aware of the crowd's eyes on Theo, the prince only had eyes for her.

They met at the edge of the dance floor.

"Hi," she said, keeping a respectable foot between them. On the inside, she was melting.

"Hi," he returned, taking her in from top to bottom and

back up. "You look gorgeous. My real life fantasy girl."

Her entire body blushed at that, heat spreading from her cheeks to her toes. "You look pretty good, yourself." Good didn't begin to cover it.

"I don't want to look anywhere else for the rest of the night."

"Theo," she whispered. It took everything she had not to reach for him. His compliments were getting harder and harder to take lightly.

"And I'm sorry, but I think probably everyone in this room now knows that."

She swallowed. Sure enough, when she glanced to the right, she found Emmaline staring at them. Crappers. She quickly turned her attention over her shoulder where it was clear from the dozens of fixed observations on Theo that he was right.

"What should we do?" she asked with barely a move of her lips. Her entire body had frozen. Could people also see how much Theo affected *her*?

"Find our table?" he suggested.

"Good idea. Hopefully, everyone will follow suit and quit looking at us."

Theo put his hand on her lower back, his warm palm meeting with her bare skin. He made a sound, something between a groan and a moan, before he leaned back just slightly and checked out her backside out of the corner of his eye. "Damn," he said under his breath.

A shiver worked its way down her spine as they made their way to where Bea and David sat with her parents. Hawk was there, too, working his charm on Bea. Nick and Cass stood nearby talking to Meg and Linc Brady. Like Rowan's brother and best friend, Meg and Linc had also gotten together after a bachelor auction.

"Hey you guys," Rowan said to the foursome. "Meg, Linc, this is Theo. Theo, Meg, and Linc Brady." Theo grinned at her before turning to Meg and Linc and shaking their hands. Oops. Was she supposed to formally introduce him? "Meg is a freelance writer for the Courier," Ro said. "When she's not busy chasing her adorable twin boys or helping Linc run their ranch."

"Sounds like you both have your hands full. What are the boys' names?" Theo asked.

The six of them continued to talk until they were kindly interrupted by guests wanting to say hello and introduce themselves to Theo. Rowan took the seat next to Hawk and watched as Theo graciously chatted with everyone and posed for pictures.

Servers filled their champagne glasses and she and Hawk toasted to the Forty-Niners making it to the Super Bowl. Theo sat beside her when dinner was served. Conversation never lagged as the table filled with the people who meant the most to her, discussed everything from her mural—she quickly changed that subject—to politics.

A few speeches followed dinner, with a special shout out

to Theo, thanking him for his generous donation to the Daughters of Montana and their endeavor to raise money for repairs to Marietta's courthouse. Rowan had no idea he'd given a gift to help commemorate the 125th anniversary of one of the town's oldest buildings. She gave his hand a squeeze underneath the table. He didn't allow her to let go, instead lacing their fingers and keeping their entwined hands on his thigh.

Music started right after that, the band opening with a waltz. Theo turned to her and said, "May I have this dance?"

"I…" The dance floor was quickly filling up, and she was quite comfortable right where she was. "I don't know how to waltz."

"The next one then," he said easily. He put his arm around her chair and canted his head until she felt his warm breath on her ear. "Fair warning, though," he added quietly. "When I hold you against me, I don't plan on letting you go."

Her stomach quivered in anticipation. She really, really wanted to bury her nose in his neck, breathe him in, and press her body to his. Desire overruled good sense and she didn't care who noticed.

Not when their eyes met and his glittered with heat. Passion. Intensity. She'd never been on the receiving end of a look like that.

She gently ran the pads of her fingers down his cheek and around his clean-shaven jaw. His face really was a work of art. "Perfect. Then I'll be right where I want to be."

He captured her wrist and brought her hand to his mouth. He kissed her knuckles, then lowered her arm, opening her fist so he held her palm face-up. With his other hand, he traced a line from the tip of her middle finger over her palm. He paused to draw lazy circles on her wrist, then continued slowly up the inside of her bare arm.

There were no words to describe how incredible that felt. She never wanted him to stop touching her. Her breasts tingled. Her stomach tightened. Her sex throbbed. And her mind was stimulated with need. Need to know every inch of his body, but also every thought in his head. Whatever this connection was between them, it took her somewhere she'd never been before, and she wanted to explore it fully.

"*Ahem.*"

Oh yeah, they weren't the only two people in the room.

Rowan pulled her arm away from Theo and turned in the direction of the throat clearing. Immediately, the haze of euphoria vanished. She straightened her back. "Hi, Emmaline."

"Rowan. Your Highness."

Theo stood, putting a hand to Ro's elbow and helping her to rise with him. "Hello, Emmaline. You look lovely this evening," Theo said.

"Thank you." She did look really pretty in her charcoal-gray dress. A touch of pink bloomed across her cheeks at Theo's compliment. "I wanted to see how your visit was going?"

"You mean how my reporter and I are getting along"—
he gave her a knowing smile—"don't you?"

"Caught," she answered cordially. "I noticed the two of
you…" She looked at Rowan with a note of caution in her
steady gaze.

"Looking too friendly?" the prince supplied.

"Frankly, yes."

"The article is finished," Rowan said. "I sent you an
email earlier to let you know you'd have it on Monday after I
do one more read through."

Emmaline's eyes widened in surprise. Rowan never finished anything early, always hitting the send key a minute
before her piece was due. Theo proved to be excellent
incentive.

"Oh, okay. Wonderful. Are you happy with it?"

"Very." She never lacked confidence with her writing,
but weirdly she hadn't felt the usual happiness with a job
done this time. She'd think about what that meant later
when she was alone.

The music changed in the background, the band rolling
over into Nat King Cole's "Unforgettable."

"Emmaline, will you excuse us? Rowan promised me the
next dance."

"Of course. Enjoy your evening." As Theo placed his
palm on her lower back and slipped behind her, Emmaline
gave her a covert wink. "Both of you."

"Thank you." Ro smiled at her boss's uncharacteristic gesture. For the first time in months, the shame Ro felt at things not going the way they should have dissipated.

Theo guided her to the dance floor. They faced each other, arms at their sides. He had to quit looking at her like she was made of stars or she'd turned to mush right there for everyone to see. His right arm went around her waist. His left hand took her right one, and he brought their laced fingers to his chest. She put her free hand on his shoulder, and they started to slow dance.

As they swayed, the air got lighter, like the two of them were inside a bubble that would float away if they lifted their feet off the floor. Theo tightened his arm around her, bringing her body closer to his. "Have I told you how beautiful you look?"

"Yes."

"Have I mentioned how sexy you are?"

"Yes." He'd whispered lots of things in her ear during dinner, making it hard to concentrate.

"And that you smell amazing." He dipped his head to her neck and inhaled.

Goose bumps rose on her flesh, and she was really glad she'd worn her hair up. His lips grazing lightly over her skin as he breathed her in set off sparks down her arms and back.

They continued to move together in perfect sync. Theo guided her around the dance floor with ease as the soft tune played for the couples lost in each other's arms. "You're unforgettable," he whispered in her ear as the song came to a close. "And that's where you'll stay," he softly crooned along with the band's singer.

Rowan bit her bottom lip to stop the onslaught of feelings rising to the surface for this incredible man. When the song ended, he looked down at her, she looked up at him, and without saying a word, they told each other how much the other meant.

Thankfully, the band picked up the pace on the next song. She and Theo danced the night away, laughing with family and friends, but not once exchanging partners. One couple in particular that Rowan met for the first time tonight, Nicki and Quincy, danced together like they'd been partnered for years. When the bandleader announced they were doing the "Cupid Shuffle" next and asked dancers to form lines, hoots and hollers sounded.

Theo gave her the cutest clueless look. "Don't worry," she said. "Just follow me." When the song kicked into high gear, Rowan lifted the hem of her red gown, followed the song's lyrics, and performed the easy dance moves beside Theo and Cassidy.

"You're wearing cowboy boots," Theo said, noticing her footwear for the first time.

"Thought I'd add a little country to the glamour." She danced right, then left, shaking her hips and drawing Theo's attention there.

Without warning, he grabbed her hand and led her off

the dance floor.

"What's wrong?" she asked, worried that maybe he'd twisted his bad ankle.

"Absolutely nothing except for the fact that I need to get you alone. Now."

Oh.

He swung by their table so she could grab her small handbag. Next, he gave his grandmother a quick kiss on the cheek, then turned to his grandfather and said "I'll get Rowan home safely."

"Goodnight," Ro called out.

They made one last stop to say goodbye to her parents, her mom beaming when Theo gave her a kiss on each cheek.

Theo's good manners had definitely put the spotlight on them now. If their families had any doubts about the two of them being more than friendly, they didn't any longer.

Coats in hand, they crossed the lobby toward the hotel's entrance. Just before stepping outside, Theo helped her into her jacket. She buttoned up and then—

He framed her face in his hands. "I can't wait another second to kiss you."

She wrapped her arms around his neck. "What are you waiting for, then?"

His slow descent contradicted his words. But as soon as he brushed his lips against hers, she understood. They only got one first kiss and the buildup was half the fun. And oh, the feather-light touch sent a burning need curling through her. "Mmm," she murmured before running her fingers through his hair and cupping the back of his head to encourage him to kiss her harder.

"God, Rowan," he hummed against her sensitive mouth before parting her lips with his tongue and plunging inside.

He tasted like chocolate and hazelnut liqueur and she wanted to feast on him for the rest of the night. His kiss…his kiss took her to another place where fireworks blazed behind her eyelids. She leaned her body into his, tangled her tongue with his. Another flash of light went off. Theo's kiss devoured her. A sharp ache settled low in her stomach. She needed him naked. Needed to touch and taste and see all of him.

An additional flash of light flared, but this time, something seemed off. An intrusion of sorts. She opened her eyes at the same time Theo did.

"Prince Theodore!" a man called out. "Who's the girl? What's it like being in your mother's hometown?" The guy took another picture with the camera around his neck. "Is this love?"

Oh my God. She wasn't seeing fireworks. It was the paparazzi.

Theo immediately shielded her from the man and hustled them out of the hotel. "I'm sorry," he said, slight panic in his tone.

The paparazzi followed several steps behind them, the flashbulb going off in rapid succession. He continued to shout questions at Theo, but Theo ignored him.

"My car is right in front," Theo said. He handed a tip to the valet, said thanks, and ushered her inside the passenger side. "Keep your head down," he directed.

She complied, a little freaked out by the strange attention. Theo scrambled into his seat a second later. Before she even had her seatbelt locked into place, he sped away from the hotel.

Once they pulled out of the parking lot and it appeared they weren't being followed, he slowed down. "You okay?" he asked, reaching over to hold her hand.

Now that they were free from unwelcome notice, she was more than okay. So okay and amused that she twisted in her seat and smiled at him. "Wow. That was an adventure. Now I know how the Kardashian's feel all the time."

He laughed. "I'm glad you're not upset."

"Why would I be upset? I got caught kissing a prince. If anything, this will raise my street value tremendously."

"Street value?"

"Yeah, I have no idea what I just said. I'm still kind of dizzy from that kiss."

That got her a bone-melting grin. "Yeah?"

"Like you don't know what a good kisser you are. I actually thought I was seeing fireworks until I realized it was a photographer snapping my picture."

Theo made an annoyed face.

"Hey," she said, leaning over to nibble his ear. "I'm fine. It's not a big deal. What is a big deal is you're taking me home. Want to sleep over?"

Chapter Eleven

ROWAN SLIPPED OFF her coat and hung it on the iron wall rack in her small entryway. She took Theo's coat and hung it up beside hers. Then she slipped her hand inside his much larger one and led him down the hallway to her bedroom. They didn't talk and the silence acted like a form of foreplay, heightening the air around them, letting her mind wander to all sorts of sexy scenarios.

All night. She had all night with him.

At her silent maneuvering, Theo sat on the upholstered bench at the foot of her bed. "Stay," she whispered into his ear.

Her sleepover. Her rules.

She'd left on the small bedside lamp, but the soft lighting wasn't enough. She wanted to feast her eyes on him, not guess, so she walked over to the standing lamp in the corner and turned it on. *Better.*

His heated gaze ate her up as she stepped back into his personal space. "The way your body moves in that dress makes me crazy," he said.

"Good crazy?" She slid her hands inside his tuxedo jacket, around his shoulders, and slowly slipped the coat down his arms, stopping halfway and trapping his arms behind him.

Excitement and I'm-game-for-whatever-you-want flashed in his eyes. "Unbelievably good."

"I like that." She undid the buttons of his white dress shirt, pressed her lips to his neck. He smelled so good she hoped his scent lingered on her skin and her sheets for days. "Know what else I like?"

"What?" he asked, his voice husky.

"You."

"I like you, too. Let me show you how much."

"After I show you." She unbuttoned the rest of his shirt. With each open clasp, she placed an openmouthed kiss to his hot, smooth skin. A light dusting of blond hair covered his muscular chest. She moved lower to hard, sculpted abs. He must do at least a thousand crunches a day. The muscles there jumped when she kissed below his belly button.

"If you're planning to continue progressing this slow, it's going to be a problem."

She'd noticed his "problem." It was *hard* not to.

"Are you laughing at me?" he goaded, his voice full of fun.

"No, no. I'm laughing at my own silly joke in my head." She put her hands on his thighs. "Sorry," she added, suddenly realizing she was nervous and *that* was why she'd decided on a slow seduction.

This night with Theo meant more than a quick trip between the sheets.

"You never have to be sorry when you're with me." His hands cupped her jawline, and he leaned forward to brush a kiss to her lips.

"You freed your arms."

"I'm taking over."

She stepped back. "*Really?*" It wasn't so much a protest as a challenge. One she had every intention of letting him win. Her rules were overrated.

He stood and shrugged out of his shirt, the material falling to the floor. She sucked in a breath, stared at all the masculine beauty before her. "I want to lick you," she blurted.

"I want to lick you, too." So he did. His lips crashed over hers, and he wasted no time licking inside her mouth.

Oh, God.

Her legs shook as the kiss deepened. She clutched his shoulders to stay upright, to anchor herself to the best thing to ever happen to her. He brought her flush against his body. His hands roamed over her bottom and up her sides before settling in her hair and pulling the pins out. The soft strands tumbled down her back. Theo groaned, kissed around her chin and down the column of her neck. His mouth set every inch of her on fire.

He made quick work of her zipper. The next thing she knew, her dress was sliding down her torso, over her hips, and landing in a pool of material at her feet.

Theo's appreciative gaze felt like a caress over her breasts, her stomach, between her thighs, and down the length of her legs. "You're magnificent."

"Right?" she teased.

His sexy smile proved a direct link to her nipples. They stiffened, ached. Taking her by the waist, he lifted her off the floor, and like she weighed nothing, playfully tossed her onto the bed.

"Hey!" She bounced before leaning back on her elbows to watch him pull a condom from his pocket, toss it beside her, and strip the rest of his clothing off. *Hello body made for unthinkable pleasure.* "I hope you brought more than one of those."

"I did."

She fell back as he crawled onto the mattress and braced all his glorious nakedness above her. His thigh nudged her legs apart. His erection pressed against her red lace panties. He kissed her, stealing her breath, before he lifted up to pierce her with dreamy blue eyes. "I'm in awe of you, Rowan Palotay," he said softly. "And plan to make love to you for the rest of the night, but right now, I want you to be a good cowgirl and ride me."

His finger hooked around the string of her panties, and he tugged them down and off. "The boots stay on." Then he flipped her on top of him so she straddled his hips.

A surge of sexual power rolled through her when she

looked down at him and saw the lust sparkling in his eyes. She rubbed her center over the hard, silky length of him until she grew wet with need. He rolled the condom on. She gripped him in her hand, and guided his tip to her opening. Then she took his hands, put them on her breasts, and sank down.

They muttered the same curse word at the sheer exquisiteness of being connected so intimately. For several pleasurable seconds she didn't move, holding on to the feel of Theo filling her so completely. They were one person. One heart. One soul. A part of each other in a way she'd never felt before. When she couldn't hold still any longer, the pleasure so intense she thought she'd come apart, she moved on him, up, down, their hips falling into a perfect rhythm. He groaned. "You feel so good," he rasped.

"So do you."

His hands played with her breasts, lightly teased and tweaked her very pert nipples. She rolled her hips forward, splayed her palms across his chest. His heart was pounding much like hers was, and the feel of its rapid beat chased away the tiny doubt that he didn't feel the same way about her that she did about him.

Their breathing quickened. The tips of his fingers slid down her sides to grip her waist. He sped up the steady tempo of their bodies by thrusting harder, faster. She arched her back and rode him with everything she had.

Could a girl die from too much pleasure? Because the

way Theo possessed her body and moved inside her was pure bliss. She shivered, imagining the other positions they'd get to. Him on top, him behind her while he bent her over the couch, her up against the wall with her legs wrapped around his hips.

They had no future together, but for tonight, he was hers and she was his.

"Theo! Oh, God, yes," she panted unable to hold off her climax any longer. "That's the spot. Right there!" She splintered in a rush of crazy good sensations that kept going. One orgasm rolled into another as Theo sat up, hugged her close, and buried his face in her neck while he followed her over the edge with a guttural groan of satisfaction.

He held her in his arms while their racing hearts slowed. She dropped her chin on his shoulder, sighed in happiness. "Wow," she said in a low voice.

"Yeah," came his gratified reply. He kissed the sensitive spot underneath her earlobe. His fingers combed through her hair at the middle of her back.

"Are you sniffing me?" She wiggled and leaned back to look at him.

"Couldn't help myself. You smell even better after sex." His smug expression implied he was taking full credit for her new and improved scent.

She tried really hard not to be affected by his overwhelming appeal, but couldn't stop the corners of her mouth from lifting while she gently brushed the hair off his forehead.

"Should we test that theory?"

"I'm very good at tests. Always ace them." He delicately traced squiggles on her lower back, making her tingle.

"I've got three more lessons planned for you then."

"Not sure that will be enough," he said. And for the rest of the night, he proved himself a master with her body.

THEO WOKE WITH Rowan's head on his shoulder, her thigh over his, and her hand resting on his stomach dangerously close to his growing erection. All it took was her breath on his chest to give new meaning to the term rise and shine. Not to mention the soft curves of her naked body curling against him were impossible to ignore. He lifted the sheet and glanced down. Yep, the tip of her finger was about to meet with the tip of his—

Before he could finish that thought, she wrapped her hand around him and stroked. "Morning," she whispered over his skin.

He mumbled something unintelligible in return. Damn, her hand felt good.

She chuckled softly before lifting up onto her elbow. "How long have you been up?" She grinned at her own joke, and he fell for her even more.

"Not long," he grunted. The woman had serious hand-job skills.

"Oh, I don't know about that. Feels long to me."

Her humor, combined with her beauty and intelligence, was ruining him in the best possible way. "Kiss me."

She scrunched up her nose. "I haven't brushed my teeth yet."

"Don't care."

"Suit yourself." She pressed her lips to his while her hand continued to pump him toward morning bliss.

The kiss started slow. A morning luxury he felt damn lucky to be on the receiving end of. When she'd confessed he was the first man to sleep in her bed overnight, he'd made sure she didn't regret it. Multiple times. He hoped to continue earning her regard for the rest of the day. He couldn't think of anything better than spending a Sunday in bed with Rowan.

Her sigh of pleasure made him even harder. He nibbled on her lush bottom lip, coaxed her lips apart so he could slide his tongue inside her mouth. More. He needed more. Seemed she did, too. She kissed him harder, poured herself into it, while at the same time rubbing him with perfect pressure. His hips bucked at the smooth glide of her palm from base to tip and back down.

He framed her face with his hands and made love to her mouth. This beautiful woman raised the stakes to a whole new level. Kissing Rowan made him want to feel things he shouldn't, but he couldn't stop himself. Here, right now, she belonged to him, and he'd make sure she knew how deep his feelings were rooted.

She broke the kiss, looked at him with glazed eyes, then sucked and licked her way down his body to take him in her mouth.

Holy hell. He cupped the back of her head, urged her to take him deeper. She did, and he was seconds away from going off. "I'm going to come," he warned. He'd be happy to push inside her and make this good for both of them. But after he felt her smile around his cock, she added that skilled hand of hers to already the best blow job of his life and his release barreled down on him. She swallowed every last drop before lifting her head and licking her lips.

"Hungry?" she asked, hopping off the bed like she hadn't just rocked his world.

All he could do was stare. With her sleep-mussed hair and supple body she wasn't shy about sharing, she triggered every possessive instinct inside him.

She grabbed a T-shirt out of her dresser, slipped it on. It barely covered the sexy curve of her butt. When she turned around, he gave her what had to be the thousandth smile since they'd met.

"It's true," she said. "Come on, let's eat some waffles."

Of Course I Talk to Myself…Sometimes I Need Expert Advice her shirt said.

He pulled on his boxer briefs and followed her into the kitchen. Snow fell outside the windows, but inside it was warm. Cozy. Watching Rowan move around the kitchen, he pictured this scenario happening on a regular basis before remembering that would be impossible.

"Can I help with anything?" he asked.

She cut him a quick glance. "That's okay. You're good right there." As if to prove that, she peeked at him—or rather his chest—often.

Silver-and-blue placemats already sat atop the round kitchen table. Rowan added plates, napkins, and utensils. "Have a seat."

He loved that she didn't ask what he liked or didn't like, that she'd decided to just feed him. She had no idea how refreshing that was. Back home no one did anything without checking with him first.

"Okay, so remember we talked about our deserted island food?" She carried two plates and a jar of what looked like peanut butter over to the table. "These are Eggos." She put everything down, and he jumped up to pull the chair out beside him. "Thank you. And this is my favorite way to eat them." On one plate were waffles. On the other were sliced bananas. "Most people like to use butter and syrup, but this is way better." She spread peanut butter on one of the waffles, added some bananas, and placed it in front of him. "Let me know what you think."

To say she was the most adorably sexy woman he had ever met would be an understatement. He waited until she had one of her own before picking up a fork and knife. When she skipped formalities and brought the waffle right to her mouth, however, he did the same.

Her eyes closed as she took a bite, chewed. "So good."

"I agree."

"Really?" Her tone indicated not too many other people agreed.

"Really." He took a second bite. And after he'd finished the first waffle, he ate a second one.

Rowan poured them orange juice. They talked about everything and nothing. Being with her was easy. He touched her often. On her arm, thigh, neck. Cupped her jaw and kissed her when she had peanut butter in the corner of her mouth. Laced their fingers together when she told him about losing her grandparents and how special Bea and David were to her.

When she stood to clean up, he grabbed her around the waist and tossed her over his shoulder.

"What are you doing? Put me down!" She wiggled and squirmed so he had no choice but to hold on to her bare bottom. "Are you copping a feel right now?"

"I plan to do more than that, princess." He carried her back to the bedroom and laid her on the rumpled bed.

She quieted, studied him with something new in the depths of her eyes, but as quickly as it had flashed, it disappeared. In an uncharacteristic move, she pulled the hem of her T-shirt down.

He hooked his arms behind her knees and tugged her to the edge of the bed, causing the shirt to ride right back up. "I can't have you covering where I want to be."

"You want to be between my legs?" Whatever momentary weirdness had just taken place vanished with her flirtatious tone of voice.

"Very much so."

She lifted her arms above her head with a dramatic sigh like he was really putting her out. "By all means then, don't let me stop you."

For the next couple of hours, they didn't. Stop. They laughed, explored each other fully, and laughed some more until they fell asleep wrapped in each other's arms.

"Hey, sleeping beauty," Theo said, roused from a very nice X-rated dream sometime later. The bedside clock read 5:35. "There's someone knocking at your door."

Rowan burrowed into the covers, made a sexy humming sound.

"Do you want me to answer it?"

"Answer what?" she mumbled.

He traced his finger over her shoulder. "Your front door. There's someone knocking."

She bolted upright. "Shit! I forgot all about my brother and Cass." She scrambled out of bed, leaned out of the room with her hands braced on the bedroom doorframe, and shouted, "Just a minute!"

Spinning around, she scanned the room. "They're here for dinner. Chinese food." She picked her T-shirt up off the floor, tugged it over her gorgeous wild mane of hair. "You're welcome to stay if you'd like. I'm sure they brought enough." Her eyes darted to his. "If you want to. No worries if you don't. I can't believe I fell back asleep for so long." She plucked underwear out of a drawer and pulled it up her legs. He envied the boy short panties.

"Either way, you need to hurry up and get dressed, please." She gathered his clothes off the floor and dumped them atop the comforter.

"I can stay." He rolled out of bed to his feet.

She looked over her shoulder, taking him in from top to bottom. "Okay. Sorry I don't have something a little more comfortable you could wear."

Another knock sounded before he could tell her no worries. "I'm surprised they haven't used their key already," she said, pulling on sweatpants and a light sweatshirt over her shirt.

"They probably noticed my rental car."

"Right." She gathered her hair and twisted it into a bun on top of her head. "Oh! I almost forgot." She hurried out of the room, but poked her head back in. "Don't worry about the snake. It's fake."

What?

"Coming!" she shouted.

Theo zipped his pants, buttoned his shirt, ran a hand through his hair, and made his way to greet her brother and best friend. He was only a couple of step behind her when she opened the front door.

"Hey guys. Sorry to keep you waiting. Come on in."

Hugs were exchanged and coats hung up before Cassidy said, "Hi" with an embarrassed grin on her face. "It's nice to see you again."

"You, too," Theo said. Cassidy and Nick were great, and he liked them. "Hey, Nick." Theo put out his hand.

"Do not say one word. I'm a grown woman," Rowan said to her brother.

Nick didn't look particularly happy to hear that or find Theo in his sister's home, but his handshake was friendly nonetheless. Theo imagined all older brothers had difficulty when their younger sisters got caught with a guy, and the thought bothered him. Despite what little time they had together, Rowan meant something to him.

"Thanks for bringing dinner over." Rowan took the large bag out of Nick's hands. "I'm starving. Come sit in the kitchen and let's dig in."

"It smells great," Theo said, falling in step behind her.

Cassidy helped Rowan set things up, moving back and forth from the kitchen table to the counter while he and Nick got comfortable in their seats. The women put their heads together to whisper and giggle more than once.

"Those two together are trouble," Nick said with affection. He'd yet to take his eyes off his fiancée.

"Rowan told me they've been friends since they were kids."

"Yeah. Once Ro lets a person inside, she keeps them there."

Good to know. Theo was the same way, but since being burned by dishonesty more than once over the past few years, he didn't let too many people get close any more. That was the one thing he envied most about his brother. Otis had found the girl of his dreams, someone to whom he could drop all his defenses and trust, and been lucky enough to marry her.

Rowan and Cassidy returned to the table with two more plates of food. Rowan was right. They had more than enough. "This is probably a dumb question, but do you have Chinese food in Montanique?" Rowan asked as she took the seat beside him.

"We do. I don't eat it very often, though, so this is nice."

"I'm glad you stuck around for it," she said.

"Me, too." He'd like to stick to her until he returned home in two weeks.

"Shoot, I forgot napkins," she said, looking around the table. "Nick, you know where they are. Would you mind grabbing us some?"

"Sure." The second Nick's back was turned, Rowan and Cassidy shared a quick mischievous look that told Theo something was up. When their attention zeroed in on Nick, Theo watched him as well.

Nick opened a kitchen drawer, looked inside, and gave a full-body startle that had him taking a step back. "Jesus Christ."

The girls burst out laughing. "Gotcha!" they said.

"You did," Nick agreed, his tone suggesting he found the situation amusing. He reached into the drawer and pulled out napkins—along with a rubber snake.

Theo chuckled. Nick tossed the snake onto the counter.

"We've had a snake war going since we were kids," Rowan told him. "Ever since Nick put one in Cass's sleeping bag because we didn't invite him to make s'mores with us."

"A real one?" Theo asked.

"It was a harmless gopher snake," Nick said with regret as he sat back down. He took Cassidy's hand and kissed her knuckles.

"It made Cass cry." Rowan's protective tone of voice once again made Theo admire her even more. These three had so much history. He wanted to hear about all of it.

"I think we need to do a reenactment," Rowan teased, standing and putting the snake back in the drawer. Then she copied her brother's movements from a minute ago, but this time, her exaggerated jump backward and squeal had Nick shaking his head in easygoing annoyance.

Rowan and Cassidy cracked up again, but Theo could tell it was all in good fun. Both women loved Nick very much.

"Payback's a bitch, ladies," Nick said with affection.

And a voice in the back of Theo's head said, *Don't let this go*. Stick around to see what Nick dished out. Theo loved being with Rowan. He could easily see himself spending much more time with her. She made him happy, turned his days into a string of unrivaled moments.

How the hell was he going to leave this girl who made him feel like no one else ever had?

Chapter Twelve

"WHAT ARE WE doing today?" Theo asked, looking impossibly sexy with wet hair, stubble on his jaw, and nothing but a towel around his waist.

Rowan should have taken much longer to walk the dogs this morning, but no, she'd hurried back to a sleeping Theo. Because…because she'd missed him. She tightened the belt on her robe and wiped the steam clouding the bathroom mirror. They'd just had shower sex. Amazing, she-left-scratches-on-his-back sex, and she needed to stop thinking about how gorgeous he was or they'd be naked again.

"*We* aren't doing anything. Since I didn't get a chance to finalize my article yesterday, I need to do it this morning and send it to Emmaline."

"Meet up with you later then?" He moved behind her to drop devastatingly sensual kisses on the side of her neck.

She involuntarily tilted her head to the side to give him full access. "Okay." She was incapable of saying no to this man.

He continued to skim his lips and tongue so affectionately over her skin that she gripped the edge of the counter to keep her legs from giving out. Theo made her feel so much it scared her.

"Have I told you how good you taste?"

"Yes," she said all breathy.

"And how good you smell?" He braced his hands beside hers, trapping her more securely between his body and the sink.

"Yes."

"There's one thing I haven't told you," he whispered behind her ear.

"What's that?" she managed to ask.

He took a step back and cool, lonely air immediately surrounded her. "I'll tell you later," he said in a seductive voice.

She swatted him on the butt as he left the bathroom. Then, because she couldn't help herself, she stood in the doorway and watched him dress.

"If you keep looking at me like that, I'm going to throw you on the bed and have my way with you again."

Sounded good to her. The feel of his chest against hers, his arms wrapped around her, his hips...

"*Rowan.*"

Work, you have to work this morning. She jerked her head to clear her thoughts. "Sorry. I'll just close the door now. See you later." She shut herself inside the bathroom and sat on the closed toilet seat.

This was bad. Really bad. She'd finally found someone she could imagine spending the rest of her life with, and he was off limits to forever. Promised to a life far away from hers. This weekend had been a mistake. He'd effortlessly wormed his way into her heart with his smile and good manners and kindness and questions and hotness, and...*ugh*.

Once she heard Theo close the front door, she left the bathroom and found he'd made the bed. Seriously? Could he stop being so perfect for one second? She settled atop the mattress with her laptop to reread her article. An hour later, she emailed it to her boss.

And an hour after that, Emmaline emailed back to tell Rowan it was her best writing yet. That should have made her jump for joy. Once the story was published, she'd be free of any remaining doubt about her integrity as a journalist and feel like she'd earned back people's respect.

Yet, she felt more relieved than anything else, happy to have the work done early. She didn't understand the change in her mindset. Since the day she'd taken over as assistant editor of her college newspaper, and their advisor had suggested she make a career out of writing, she'd thought of little else. Laying her head on her pillow and closing her eyes, though, she thought back on the past few years. Specifically, the dream she'd never allowed herself to take seriously because of fear. Fear of failing something that made her feel more alive than anything else.

She slid out of bed and cleaned her house. Nothing like sweeping and dusting to get a girl's mind off her troubles.

There was also nothing like a knock on the front door to

relieve her of the domestic duties.

"Hi," she said to Theo, surprised and foolishly happy by his appearance. She'd assumed his "later" meant tonight, but apparently in prince lingo it meant a few hours. "Whatcha got there?" In one arm, he held a large bag from her favorite art store, and in the crook of his other, he had two square canvases.

She swallowed the knot of emotion in the back of her throat.

"I was hoping you could teach me to paint," he said, stepping inside. He headed straight for the kitchen where he put the bag atop the table and the canvases on a chair before hanging his coat over the back of an empty chair and turning to her. "Hi." His lips were on hers a second later, his hands cupping her neck.

Lifting on tiptoes, she kissed him back. Gently slid the black beanie off his head so it fell to the floor and ran her fingers through his hair.

They'd kissed *a lot* over the past couple of days, but something about this kiss touched her in a different way. Like Theo cherished her. She opened her eyes and broke their connection before devotion snared her for good.

"Paint, huh?" She took a steady breath, moved around him to pick up his beanie and look inside the bag.

"You told me you took classes as a kid where they showed you some shortcuts." That he remembered the things she'd shared made her want to confess more to him. "And you're a thousand times more talented now, so I thought perhaps we could draw something together, then I could gift mine to my grandparents."

Rowan looked over her shoulder at him. Affection colored his blue eyes, but more than that, she saw respect. He had no idea how much his bringing painting into her home and wanting her to share it with him meant. No one had ever done something like this for her before.

"What did you have in mind?" She pulled the art supplies out of the bag.

He took the spot beside her, their arms brushing. Even through their clothing, the contact sent warm sensations through her. "Something easy. Trees. A mountain. Frozen pond."

"You want to paint Marietta at Christmas time."

"That's a great idea."

She bumped his shoulder. "Your great idea and I think Bea and David will love it. Has anyone ever told you you're kind of awesome?" A gift like this would mean the world to his grandparents. He hadn't come straight out and said it, but he wanted to paint Miracle Lake, the place that had meant something special.

"My mom," he said in answer to her question, the mood turning more serious.

"She'd be extremely proud of you right now. I'm sure she hung up pictures you drew as a kid, right?"

"Not really. I didn't draw keepsakes very often." He eyed

the paints, then picked up a package of brushes to open.

"Too busy playing with cars and trucks?" She walked to the closet in the hallway and pulled out the two easels she had.

Theo watched her set them up side by side and place a canvas on each. "I did do that, but more so it's because when I was young I was much more an auditory learner than a visual one. The way I perceived shapes and things was different from other kids so I got teased a lot for my drawings. I avoided art after that, until with enough practice at home with my mom, I learned to draw like everyone else.

She wrapped her arms around his waist and hugged him tightly. It meant a lot that he'd shared that. All these glimpses into his life made it harder and harder to keep her heart closed off. "Well, in case you haven't noticed, I hate doing things like everyone else so our paintings are going to be spectacular no matter what."

"Has anyone ever told you you're kind of awesome?"

Rowan gave him a quick smile and kiss. "Let's do this."

They painted together using the visual-spatial organization skills Rowan remembered learning as a child. She took her time, painting the desired shape first, then waiting for Theo to copy her. He did really well filling the 11x17 canvas with his own unique touch.

"If you brush more like this," she said, wrapping her hand around his to help him tweak his brush stroke, "the pine trees will look a little more three dimensional."

There was nothing intimate about what they were doing, but painting together with her hand clasped over his connected them in a way she never had with anyone else. Her deepest unspoken feelings surfaced when she painted and to share this was a big deal. Heart pounding, she closed her eyes for a second.

"Thanks," he said, seemingly oblivious to her internal freak out. "Can I ask you something?"

Theo learned quickly so she pulled her hand back and resumed work on her own painting. "Sure."

"What made you decide to work for a newspaper?"

"I like to write and I've always been good at telling stories."

"You're good at a lot of things." He dipped his brush for more paint.

"Why thank you, Your Highness."

"But you're exceptional at painting. Why not pursue it? I haven't read your writing, but I have seen your mural." He paused and admired her painting. "And that"—he pointed his brush at the canvas—"is remarkable. It makes mine look like—"

"Hey, this is a criticism-free zone, mister. Your painting looks great for a novice."

"I have a good teacher." He continued to watch her paint rather than resume his own work. "So?"

"So, like I told you before, I enjoy it as a hobby." She kept her attention on painting. If she turned to him, she worried he'd see how her answer didn't ring completely true.

"Tell me how you really feel."

"I just did."

"No." He gently took her chin and turned her head so their eyes met. "Tell me how you really feel, Ro."

She dropped her arm, put her paintbrush down. He'd never called her Ro before. Her stomach fluttered. And damn him, he wasn't oblivious to her true feelings. She hadn't thought it possible in such a short time, but she didn't just *like* this amazing man. She loved him.

Which was damn inconvenient.

She gave him her back in order to take a minute to compose herself. No way did she want him noticing *that*.

He gave her maybe thirty seconds before he put his hands on her waist and whispered, "I'm sorry. I didn't mean to upset you."

"You didn't." He'd done everything but that. Could she get out the truth and really answer his question as he'd asked? A big part of her wanted to. Wanted to say out loud what she'd kept buried deep in her heart.

She turned and met his warm, compassionate gaze like he needed to *see* she wasn't upset. "It's just no one has ever asked me that." She leaned into his touch when he ran the back of his hand softly across her cheek.

"Which is how I've wanted it. Pretending my art doesn't mean as much as it does is easier than putting myself out there when I already have a job I'm good at."

He tugged her to a chair at the table and sat her down on his lap. "What if pretending is interfering with the person you're meant to be?" he said with kindness, deference.

Rowan wrapped her arms around him and buried her face in his neck, overcome with emotion. Theo hugged her close, making her feel safe. Cared for. Being with him changed so many things inside her.

"I never thought of it that way," she whispered.

"Maybe you should."

"Maybe I should," she echoed before lifting her head and staring into his bottomless blue eyes. "Have I told you that you have a way with words?"

"Coming from a writer, I'll take that as a huge compliment." He gently rubbed up and down her back.

"I believe you owe me one more confession. Something you promised you'd tell me later?"

"That's right. Have I mentioned how much I like to *show* and *tell*?" He stood with her cradled in his arms and carried her toward the bedroom.

"You haven't," she said coyly.

"Let's get on that right away, then."

She shivered with anticipation. "If we must."

He paused mid-step. "The painting can wait, right?"

"For this? Definitely." Truth be told, nothing felt more right than what they were about to do.

THEO LAID ROWAN down on the bed. He palmed the back of her head to slant her mouth to his liking, then kissed her with everything he had inside him so she'd know right now she belonged to him. He slid his other hand to her perfectly round bottom, cupped it, and brought her closer. He always wanted her closer.

She set his blood on fire with a simple touch. Made every possessive bone in his body hers when she let her defenses down and talked to him. Her vulnerability turned him on at the same time it stoked his desire to take care of her.

"Theo," she murmured, biting his lower lip. She clutched his shirt and pulled, her eagerness to get it off him leading to a frantic tugging and removing of clothing until only Ro's blue-trimmed boy cut panties remained. She looked hot as hell in them and nothing else.

Straddling her thighs, he took a minute to enjoy the view of flushed, soft skin, her round breasts and pretty pink hardened nipples, the way her eyes seemed to go from blue to gray when she was aroused.

"You're not just going to stare at me, are you? Because if that's the case, I'll give you something to look at." She traced a finger down her neck toward the middle of her chest, while her other hand slid down her stomach and over her panties.

As tempting an offer as that was, he had other things on his mind. He'd watch her next time. God, he wanted a thousand next times with her.

He took her wrist, kissed the inside of her palm, and lifted her arm over her head. She voluntarily reached up with her other arm, surrendering to him, giving him carte blanche to do whatever he wanted. "I want *my* hands on you," he growled.

"I love your hands on me."

"Where? Where do you love them?" He skimmed a hand over her breast, down her stomach. Toyed with the edge of her panties.

"Everywhere." She arched her back, undulated her hips.

She was so unbelievably gorgeous, he *could* stare at her all day, every day. He tucked his hand inside her panties and watched her lips part with a sigh of pleasure.

He'd never wished so hard for things to be different. He wanted to tell her he could see himself doing this for the rest of his life. No one made him feel the way she did. He wanted to tell her he'd give up everything for her. But he didn't because it scared him to have feelings like that.

You love her.

"Theo." Her hushed husky voice brought him back, and he couldn't linger any longer. He lowered his head and kissed the hell out of her. Then hands and mouths seeking and devouring, they made each other feel so good, he was out of his mind with lust. Just before he thrust inside her, their fingers laced together above her head, he looked into her eyes and gave her that last admission.

"You're the best thing that's ever happened to me," he said in a low voice. "And I won't ever forget our time together."

Her gaze held his. "I won't either."

For the rest of the afternoon, they didn't use words to express their feelings, but actions that left them breathless, satiated, and smiling. When sometime later, they returned to the kitchen to finish their paintings, Theo wondered for the hundredth time how he was going to leave her.

"That looks great," she said, dipping her fork into a container of leftover Chinese food. "Now you just need to sign your name at the bottom and you're done."

He signed "TC" then took a step back to check out his work. It didn't compare to Ro's, but it wasn't half bad.

"I promise this will be the best Christmas present they've ever received." She kissed his cheek to bolster her compliment.

"Who are you going to give yours to?" He took a seat at the table and picked up the bowl of fried rice.

She leaned over from the chair next to his and poked her fork into his rice. He loved that she seemed to like whatever he had more than her own choosing. "I thought I'd give it to you." She dropped her gaze to the table. "If you want it. You don't have to accept it. I'm sure it doesn't match your décor at home, but it's a little slice of Marietta you can take with you. I won't know what you do with it, so if you just want to stick it in a closet or something you—"

He cut her off by claiming her mouth with a kiss that hopefully left no doubt he appreciated the gift. "Thank you."

Every time he looked at the painting, he'd think of her.

She caught her breath, her lips swollen from his taking. "You're welcome."

"You're cute when you're nervous. I don't think I've heard you ramble like that before." To see all the sides of Rowan softened his heart in the way he'd reserved only for his mom.

"Because I don't normally get nervous," she said with sass before stuffing her face with more food.

He joined her in eating to avoid further discussion. These feelings were emotions he couldn't keep no matter how much he might want to.

"I forgot to ask, did I leave my phone here?" He'd had it in his pocket Saturday night at the ball, but hadn't seen it since.

"You did. Sorry I forgot to mention it sooner. I found it under my bed when I was cleaning earlier. I'll grab it for you." She left the room and returned with his cell.

"Thanks." Glancing at the screen, he had several missed calls and texts from his father and brother. Shit. Had something happened? It was too late back home to call his dad, but he could wake up Otis.

"Is everything okay?" Rowan asked.

"I don't know. I need to call my brother." He tapped the screen and waited for his brother to pick up.

"Hey, Theo. About time I heard back from you," Otis said, his voice groggy from sleep.

"I misplaced my phone. What's going on? Is Dad all right?" Theo kept eye contact with Rowan as he spoke.

"That depends. Did you read his texts?"

"No, I rushed to call you instead. Talk to me already."

"You've made international news with your new lady love, and Dad is pissed," his brother said, sounding more awake now.

"Back up. What are you talking about?"

"You and a hot brunette in a red dress playing tonsil twister. I take it she was your reporter?"

Theo squeezed his eyes shut. Damn it. The paparazzi Saturday night had taken pictures of him and Rowan. At the time, it hadn't occurred to him the photo would make the news. He explained the situation to Otis, who told him he was an idiot not to have Hawk with him at all times. His brother didn't get it, though. Marietta wasn't that kind of place. "Is Rowan's name mentioned?" He met her wide eyes.

"What fun would that be? It's much more interesting to speculate and make crap up. And besides, there's no clear shot of her face."

"They left your name out," he told her.

"She's there with you?" Otis asked, surprise and curiosity in his voice. "Want to tell me what's going on? You sounded awfully relieved *and* smitten just now."

"Later," Theo said firmly. "How upset is Dad?"

"Upset enough that he wants you home yesterday."

Theo scrubbed a hand down his face. "And if I refuse?"

He wasn't ready to leave his grandparents. Wasn't ready to leave Rowan.

"Said the good son only once before. You must really like this girl. Tell you what, I'll do what I can on my end since I know you wanted to be there for Christmas, but Dad…"

"Dad what?"

"He's really feeling your absence, and Christmas Day is going to be tough on him given it would have been mom's fiftieth."

Something must have shown on Theo's face because Rowan reached across the table and placed her palm atop his, then rubbed her thumb across his skin.

His chest ached for the loss his family had suffered and for the loss he'd feel when he said goodbye to his grandparents and Rowan.

If there was ever a time for a Christmas miracle, it was now.

"I'll call Dad in the morning," Theo said.

"Good. Touch base with me afterward, okay?" The sound of Otis yawning came across the phone line.

"Yeah. Go back to sleep. Sorry I woke you." Theo signed off and put his phone on the table, his thoughts spiraling in a million different directions.

Rather than ask him any questions, Rowan stood and straddled his lap. She framed his face in her soft hands, looked deep into eyes, and kissed him. The gentle press of her lips turned into a wild tangle of tongues when he swept his hands all over her body. He couldn't keep his hands to himself when she was near. And right now, he needed to forget.

They kissed for a long time, and Theo sensed this might be the last time they held each other like this. He deepened the kiss. When they needed to come up for air, Rowan put her hands on the nape of his neck. From her pained expression, he'd swear she was about to tell him good-bye.

"I've never put my heart in someone else's hands," she admitted, a nervous edge to her voice. "But it's in yours and I don't like losing control like this, so please don't say anything, just show me that maybe you feel the same way, too, before you…"

Leave.

Whether he liked it or not, stayed the ten more days or left tomorrow, this *was* goodbye. There was so much to say to her, but she'd asked him not to. He sealed his mouth over hers, lifted her into his arms, and carried her to the couch in the other room where he could make love to her alongside the glow from the tiny white lights on the Christmas tree. *You own my heart, too, Rowan Palotay.*

And he feared she always would.

Chapter Thirteen

ROWAN COULDN'T GET last night out of her head. The way Theo had worshipped her body had definitely felt a lot like…more than just sex. But then, it had never felt just like sex between them. They'd gotten to know each other really well before they'd even shared their first kiss, and that foundation made intimacy between them that much stronger. As soon as she'd confessed he had her heart, though, she'd wanted to swallow back the words. Say, "kidding!" and have a food fight or something. Because how ridiculous was that? He had a life far away from her small town. But he'd kissed her, taken her in his arms, and laid her on the couch next to the Christmas tree, and she forgot about her unease.

Forgot about everything except the two of them. When he quietly dressed and left, she blinked away the tears threatening to spill down her cheeks. She only cried at weddings. And during that television commercial where the boy was throwing out the first pitch at a baseball game and the catcher turned out to be his father who was stationed overseas and wanted to surprise his son. Tear jerker, that one.

After she'd gotten her emotions under control, she'd hopped on the Internet to check out the damage she'd caused. Photos of her and Theo kissing in the lobby of the Graff were everywhere, along with speculation and not-so-flattering headlines.

No wonder Theo's dad was upset. Not exactly the type of images he'd want circulating only weeks before announcing his son's engagement. To another woman.

To the right kind of woman. Not Elisabeth, but someone else royal and beautiful, no doubt.

Rowan wasn't under any delusions. She knew what she and Theo had didn't include a happily ever after. But that hadn't stopped her from falling for him. And it didn't help the sting of feeling like she'd made another mistake. This time hurting someone she loved. Theo's eyes had been tortured as he spoke to his brother, and she hated that so, so much. As close as Theo had been to his mother, he was loyal and faithful to his father, too, and he'd inadvertently hurt him. Because of his involvement with her.

Thankfully, she didn't think anyone in Marietta had seen the pictures since no one had mentioned it. Standing in her parents' kitchen for the last two hours baking gave her mom and Cassidy ample time to bring it up, and they hadn't.

Then again, they knew her well enough to know she was beating herself up over the situation all on her own. The only saving grace was her name hadn't been included.

A dish towel hit Rowan in the face.

"Hey!"

"Earth to Rowan," Cass said good-naturedly. "You've rolled out that dough to oblivion."

Rowan looked down. Yep, she had. She put the rolling pin aside and patted the sugar cookie dough back into a disc.

"How about I do that and you just decorate? You are the one with the awesome art skills." Cass slid the parchment paper with the dough away and put one of the wire racks with cooled cookies in front of her. This batch was shaped like snowflakes.

"And while you're doing that, spill whatever's on your mind," Ro's mom said.

"You guys know what's on my mind." She grabbed the white icing. "But let's change the subject."

"We haven't yet started on the subject," her mom said.

Silence filled the room. Ro had enough of the subject in her head to keep them on it for days. But she wasn't ready to discuss Theo yet.

So instead, she blurted out, "I want to paint." She'd hoped the admission meant she could avoid talking about her love life, but she also wanted to get this huge, scary desire off her chest and see what her mom and best friend thought.

"Finally," they said in unison.

Rowan lifted her head from her task to find both women with their arms crossed and warm smiles on their faces. She had no idea what her expression said, but the three of them were hugging a second later.

"Tell us more," her mom said, stepping to the oven and pulling out two more cookie sheets. When Shari Palotay baked Christmas cookies, she made *a lot* of them. The house smelled like sugar and butter and deliciousness for days afterward.

"You think it's a good idea that I pursue painting?"

"I think it's always best to follow your heart. When you're blessed with an exceptional gift that compliments your dream, nothing should stop you from going for it." Spoken like the awesome mom Shari was.

"Why didn't you ever say anything to me?"

"When have you followed any suggestion I've made? In fact, you usually do the opposite. You've been headstrong and stubborn since you were a toddler, and if something isn't your idea, you rarely follow through."

Rowan watched her mom slide each freshly baked cookie onto a wire rack as she let those words sink in. They were true. "So you've been waiting for me to come to the conclusion on my own," Ro stated.

"Your father had to sit on me more than once to keep me from coming to the hospital to see you working on the mural and tell you painting was your passion, not writing." She pointed the spatula in her hand at Rowan. "Although you are an excellent writer, too."

"I've got a couple of contacts I could hook you up with," Cassidy said. "On a lot of my shoots, we need something painted on the side of a building, or even some funky paint job done to a car. You could create a really cool niche for yourself if you wanted to, and keep writing to pay the bills until your new career takes off."

Rowan braced her hands on the counter. Money had been one of her main concerns. Could she do both things and not starve?

"Okay," she said. Simple as that, yet she knew it wouldn't be easy.

Cass squealed. Her mom clapped like Ro had taken first place in a national contest.

"But let's keep this between us until I figure everything out."

"You know your father and I are here if you need any—"

"No. You guys have done enough. I need to do this on my own." At her mom's dropped head, Rowan added, "But thank you. I know you and Dad have my back, and that's a good feeling."

Ro's cell phone chimed with a text, drawing her attention to the kitchen table. She walked over to read the message.

Hi Rowan, give me a call or text back when you have a chance. Thanks, Theo

She put the phone down and turned back around with no intention of calling or texting. She didn't want him to know how much his leaving was affecting her, so she'd decided to keep her distance. Maybe that made her a coward.

But she wanted to keep last night as her final memory because she had a strong hunch he'd be returning home in the next couple of days.

"Was that Theo?" Cass asked sweetly.

"Yes."

"Making more plans?"

Ro shrugged. She usually told Cass everything, but this time, she couldn't muster her usual indifference, which left her tight lipped for the first time ever. She'd give her best friend all the details later, after Theo had returned home and the ache in her chest wasn't so sharp.

"Looks like I got here at the perfect time," Nick said, walking into the kitchen and wrapping Cassidy in a hug from behind. He reached around her to steal a finished cookie off the counter.

"Hey, mister," their mom said as he put the entire cookie in his mouth. "These are for Christmas Eve. I've got other cookies you can have now."

"Sorry," he said with his mouth full.

He'd done the same thing as a boy. Ever since Ro could remember, her mom had baked and decorated sugar cookies for Christmas. And Nick always took one when he wasn't supposed to. She inwardly smiled and got back to decorating the snowflake cookies, but out of the corner of her eye, she noticed the affection between Nick and Cass as he "helped" her roll out the dough, and the happy expression on her mom's face.

Family meant everything.

Theo felt the same way. Which was why he'd fly home to take his place beside his father and brother as soon as possible. Rowan could never fault him for that.

THEO JAMMED HIS fingers through his hair. It had been a long day. First, he'd called Elisabeth. She confirmed she was pregnant and planned to marry her boyfriend. Her parents were supportive of the change in plans. "What's up with you and the girl in the red dress?" she'd asked. "Is she someone special?" Theo said yes, and asked about the gossip back home. "It's nothing you can't handle," she'd answered. Which told him nothing.

Second, he'd called his father. His dad had a way of keeping his voice calm, but making it known he was unhappy as hell. Theo didn't go into details about his relationship with Rowan. He did go into details about Elisabeth. They talked for a long time after that, discussing other marriage options before Theo managed to turn the conversation to the last Council of State meeting and his father's acceptance of several invitations for upcoming exhibitions and anniversaries. His dad's voice had turned decidedly melancholy then, twisting Theo's stomach into a tight knot. The king was counting on Theo and Otis now more than ever to attend events with him.

Hoping to end their phone call on a happier note, Theo

told his dad about Bea and David and the small town his mom had once called home. His dad sounded genuinely happy that Theo had taken this opportunity, but asked him to come home early. A lengthy conversation with Otis in which Theo reiterated the discussion with their father followed.

Next, Theo finalized arrangements for the bench being gifted to Marietta, grateful everyone could change the date of delivery.

Travel arrangements followed.

Two days. He had two days left in Marietta. That got him home in time for Christmas and gave him the opportunity to fulfill his promise to his grandparents: Christmas dinner, albeit early. And he'd be here for the small dedication ceremony when the bench was placed at Miracle Lake.

He laid his head back on the leather couch.

"I finally got Mabel to give me a smile. My work here is done," Hawk said, striding into the sitting room of the bed and breakfast and taking his usual spot near the fireplace.

"I guess now would be a bad time to tell you she smiled at me last week?" Mabel Bramble, owner of the B&B, had a crusty exterior, but deep down, Theo suspected she hid a marshmallow center.

"Whatever." Hawk put his legs up on the coffee table. "You look like you could use a beer. Or three."

"Sounds like a plan. You buying?"

"Already have a six pack in the fridge. Thought we'd order burgers and onion rings from Grey's Saloon to go with."

Theo raised his brows. "Aren't you the know-it-all?" Rowan had driven him by Grey's, but that's as close as he'd gotten.

"Kept myself busy while you did the same. Speaking of which, have you heard back from her?"

"No." He'd called and texted Rowan to no avail. They'd sort of said goodbye last night, but it didn't seem right to leave it at that. His fault. He'd walked out after the most intense sex of his life.

"You think she's ghosting you?" Hawk said like that was something funny.

"I have no idea what that means." Hawk loved to call him out on his lack of knowledge with American slang words and phrases.

Hawk waved his arm in the air. "It's nothing." He leaned forward, elbows on his knees. His expression turned serious. "But maybe she's trying to tell you she's done."

Theo let out a deep breath. "Probably for the best." Only it felt like the worst possible thing to happen to him. To never see her again. Touch her. Hear her laugh. His heart would never fully recover from the loss.

"How about I grab another six pack when I pick up the food?"

Getting drunk sounded a lot better than staying sober at the moment. "Now you're talking my language." Hawk was good people. The best. "Thanks, man."

The next day, however, Theo sat at the large wooden breakfast table across from Hawk and said, "The next time you add a bottle of Jack to our beers, I'm going to have to fire you."

Hawk laughed, not the least bit hung over this morning, the bastard. "Noted."

Theo squeezed his temples, hoping to alleviate the throbbing in his head. Didn't help. Eliza's home cooking might, though. She carried two plates piled with gingerbread pancakes that smelled out of this world.

"Good morning, gentlemen," she said. At Hawk's request, she'd been kind enough to extend the breakfast hour from nine to eleven in order for Theo to sleep in.

"Morning," he and Hawk said. "Thank you for the late breakfast," Theo added.

"Since it's just the two of you, it's no bother. I am sad to see you leave tomorrow, though. It's been an honor having you stay with us."

"I've greatly enjoyed being here." Theo gave her a smile, then dug into his pancakes.

After breakfast, he and Hawk did some shopping around town and drove to Miracle Lake to meet with the mayor and a few others to decide the exact placement of the bench so the snow could be cleared. The weather forecast called for sunny skies today and tomorrow, but the icy air kept their meeting brief.

By late afternoon, they were on their way to Bea and David's house for dinner. As they approached Rowan's cottage, Theo asked Hawk to stop. His reason was twofold. To see her and to pick up the painting he'd done.

His heart hammered inside his chest as he knocked on her front door. When she didn't answer, he peered inside the front window. The white lights on the Christmas tree glowed, but other than that, the house looked vacant.

"Meet you up there," Theo called to Hawk through the open passenger window. "I'm going to walk." And get his shit together before he saw Bea and David. God, he missed Rowan.

Snow covered the ground in a white blanket that glittered with the setting sun.

Trees loomed taller than the giants of his childhood imagination.

He paused to take it all in, breathe the scents of pine, wood, and chimney smoke. The stillness and beauty awed him every time.

Hawk waited for him at the front door of his grandparents' house with the gifts they'd purchased today. Theo rang the doorbell and opened the unlocked door. "Hello?" he called out.

His grandmother greeted them with hugs and kisses to each cheek. "I'm so happy to see you both. Come in, come in."

"We've got a few things for under the Christmas tree," Theo said.

"You didn't need to do that. Rowan was already here and

dropped off the special gift she said you had for us."

"Rowan was here?" Theo gave himself a mental slap. His grandmother had said that quite plainly.

Bea put her hand on his cheek. "She left about an hour ago. I asked her to stay for dinner, but she had other plans."

"With her family?" he asked. Why, he didn't know. He needed to drop it. Move on.

"She didn't say. Let's get your coats off." She sweetly helped them like they were young boys. "Now go ahead and put those gifts under the tree and come sit down. Dinner is ready and your grandfather is starving."

Hawk followed Bea while Theo placed the presents beside a couple of others. Rowan had wrapped his painting in colorful holiday paper and included a large red bow. Once again, she'd taken care of someone other than herself. He'd like to tell her thank you, but his gut told him it was too late for that. Sure enough, his eye caught on another large package in the corner of the room, this one wrapped in thick brown packing paper.

He stepped closer. He knew what it was. Rowan had written his name on a small envelope attached to the upper left hand corner. He carefully pulled the card off and slid out the note. *Merry Christmas, Theo.*

Three words. That was all she'd given him. He had a damn encyclopedia of words to say to her. When she cut the strings, she severed them with a sharp knife, leaving no doubt she wanted to be left alone.

Fine. He could do that.

Chapter Fourteen

T HE NEXT DAY, Theo and Hawk arrived at Miracle Lake to find a huge throng of people. "So much for a small gathering," Hawk said, putting his hand on Theo's shoulder. "It looks like the whole town is here."

"Yeah." Theo took a minute to look out the passenger window before exiting the car, a little too choked up to move just yet. He scanned the crowd, foolishly looking for one face in particular, but he didn't find her.

Hawk opened his door, always knowing when he needed to be a step ahead. "It's a nice send off."

"Yes it is." And if he didn't get out of the car and get the ceremony going, he and Hawk would be late for their flight home. Theo pulled himself together and met his friend at the side bumper.

On the walk to the site by the frozen pond where the bench had been placed, Theo shook hands with the towns-people. He thanked them for coming out on this sunny, but cold winter day. He posed for pictures and selfies. Being in the public eye was a big part of his life and he enjoyed it on days like today. Other times, not so much.

Once again, he scanned the crowd for Rowan. He caught sight of his grandparents, Eliza and her husband Marshall, Rowan's parents, and many others he'd met over the past weeks. But no sign of the gorgeous woman he couldn't get out of his head.

Which was for the best. Seeing her would only make leaving more difficult.

"Your Highness," Emmaline said, coming to walk beside him and Hawk.

He smiled. "Hi. This is a great turn out. I didn't expect quite so many people."

"I put a small notice in the paper yesterday. I hope you don't mind. But it's not every day our town is honored with a gift from a royal family."

When Theo's mom had requested he visit Marietta, she'd also asked him to give a gift to the town. A bench at Miracle Lake, she'd said, to let them know though she'd never returned home, she'd always kept her hometown close to her heart.

"I'm honored, too. Truly."

"We love you, Prince Theodore!" girls shouted from his left.

He turned and smiled, waved to the group of people since he had no idea who had called out. For a second, he thought he saw a familiar mane of dark hair, but when the woman's face came into clear view, he didn't recognize her.

Theo and Hawk arrived at the iron bench facing the lake.

His grandmother, eyes damp with tears, wrapped her arms around him. "It's beautiful," she said.

His grandfather hugged him next. No words were spoken, but then they didn't need to be. Theo could see how choked up David was, that this bench meant more to him than anyone realized.

"I hope you'll come sit here and think of her," Theo said for David's ears only.

The older man cleared his throat and nodded.

Brief speeches were given before Theo spoke a few words about his mom, his grandparents, and the town he'd come to love. "Thank you for making me feel like I belonged here. And thank you for giving my mother a wonderful childhood she always remembered with great fondness and love," he said in closing.

Applause rang out, and then Theo cut the red ribbon stretching from one arm of the wrought iron bench to the other. In the center of the backrest, the silver plaque read:

In loving memory of Her Majesty, The Queen of Montanique
Ashlyn Owens Chenery was here.

Theo grinned. His mom had a wonderful sense of humor and had requested any official sign be fun, not stuffy. He looked briefly up to the blue sky. She'd like this.

The crowd dispersed, some leaving, others taking a closer look at the bench and having a seat. Theo spent the last few minutes saying goodbye. Rowan's parents told him what a pleasure it was to meet him and not to be a stranger. Eliza told him and Hawk the B&B was theirs any time they wanted it and not to be a stranger. Emmaline thanked him for being interviewed and promised to forward him Rowan's story. She, too, told him not to be a stranger.

Turning to his grandparents, his heart thudded inside his chest. "I'll be back," he told them, but the three of them knew he might…not. Theo hated to think he wouldn't be, but his reality meant he didn't always get to do what he wanted.

His grandmother's tears killed him. "I love you very much," she told him.

"I love you, too," he said.

"We'll see each other again," David said, his voice cracking. "And we'll keep in touch."

That Theo could do. Would do.

"We need to go," Hawk said.

One more round of hugs followed, including Hawk this time, and everyone dispersed. "Give me a minute," Theo said when they got to the car.

"We really need to hit the road, Your Highness." Hawk meant serious business when he formally addressed Theo.

"Understood." He quickly walked through the snow toward the frozen lake. He needed to have his feet in the powder one more time. Look out at the scenery and inhale the scents. Remember the sleigh ride and everything else he and Rowan had done.

He turned to go back to the car, but something in the smooth snow caught the corner of his eye. Writing. He stepped closer to the indentations where someone had written *Live the life you want to live* with a stick, he guessed.

Theo almost fell to his knees as the memory of what his mom whispered to him came flooding back. She'd said those exact words to him shortly before she died. *This is impossible.* He looked around to find someone holding a stick, but he was completely alone.

"Your minute's up!" Hawk shouted out of sight.

Was Theo just supposed to leave after seeing this? His father's words echoed in his head. *I miss you, son, and need you home.*

Damn it. He trudged back to the car; his muscles bunched tight, his throat dry, his thoughts disjointed.

"You okay?" Hawk asked, looking him in the face when he took the passenger seat.

"Yeah."

They drove in silence toward the airport some thirty-five miles away in Bozeman. Theo wasn't sure how much time had passed, it could have been five minutes or it could have been three hours. Didn't matter. "Turn the car around!"

"Jesus," Hawk said, fumbling with the steering wheel for a moment. "You scared the shit out of me. What are you talking about?"

"Turn the car around. I love her."

Hawk grinned, slowed the car, and made a U-turn right there in the middle of the highway.

"My father married the woman of his dreams," Theo said. "Granted, his father had passed and he had no one but himself to answer to, but if my mother were here, she'd want me to follow my heart. She'd want me to live the life *I* want to live, and she'd make my dad see that.

"How can he fault me for following the same course he did? I can't believe I didn't think of that before. I should have told him I loved her; that I'm twenty-eight years old and I can, and will, make my own decisions. I'll always do my best for my country and for him, but I'm allowed to put myself first. I don't want my heart spared. I want it in Rowan's hands."

"You have a plan?" Hawk asked. "To win back the girl?"

Theo put his elbow on the passenger door windowsill, his head in his hand. An idea came to him that he hoped proved how serious he was about her. They had a lot to figure out, but there was no one else he wanted to share his future with.

"I have the perfect plan."

Rowan stood behind the crowd and watched Theo. She wore her white ski jacket, mirrored sunglasses, and had her hair bundled up underneath her white knit cap. As far as disguises went, so far, so good. It didn't hurt that all eyes were on the prince. They were always on the prince.

Hers included.

She couldn't help herself even though it hurt so badly to look at him.

No way would she miss this important event, though. It meant a lot to Bea and David. To the town. And to Theo, by the gracious and responsive look on his handsome face.

He posed for pictures, shook hands, and chatted with everyone who wanted a word with him.

Rowan had taken a look at the bench earlier, before the majority of people arrived. She'd chuckled when she read the plaque and looked forward to settling her bottom on the seat with a cup of hot chocolate in her hand sometime soon. When it didn't kill her to think about Theo.

"Thank you for making me feel like I belonged here. And thank you for giving my mother a wonderful childhood she always remembered with great fondness and love," Theo said.

Ro wiped the tear at the corner of her eye. She needed to leave before she did something crazy like run to him and what? They couldn't be together no matter how she looked at it.

As the crowd scattered and Theo said his goodbyes, Rowan took a little walk around the frozen lake on her way to her car. Thoughts of Theo weren't the only thing filling her head. Painting and the next step to making her true dream a reality were, too. She picked up a lone stick lying in the snow. The long, smooth branch reminded her of an old-fashioned writing instrument.

Live the life you want to live, she wrote in the snow.

She wanted to paint murals and anything and everything else she could to make a difference. Children's hospitals topped her list. She could stay with her brother and Cass in Los Angeles. Had friends in Seattle and Wyoming. And she hoped to have more opportunities right here in Marietta.

Whatever life brought her, she planned to embrace it, not hide from it. If she respected her talents, other people would, too.

When she got home, she changed into a long-sleeved T-shirt and yoga pants. This afternoon, she'd promised herself a relaxing day in front of the television since tomorrow started three days of Christmas celebrating with her family. She had a couple of gifts left to wrap, but she'd do them later.

She made herself some hot apple cider and turned on the Christmas tree lights. Once settled onto the couch, she hit the movie jackpot with *The Holiday*. Jude Law looked especially handsome in this movie, so he'd definitely keep her attention.

Sometime later, though, she was startled awake by a firm knock on the front door. She yawned, stretched, and by the new movie on the television screen, had been asleep for a while. Jude had totally failed, but she had gotten some much-needed rest after a few restless nights of sleep.

She padded to the door and opened it, thinking it was probably Cass stopping by, but instead, the sexiest man alive greeted her. "*Theo?*"

"Hi, Rowan."

"Is everything okay? What are you doing here? Is it Bea or David?" Panic scratched the back of her throat. "Did something happen?" Surely it had to be something serious to have Theo standing on her porch. Wasn't he supposed to be on an airplane by now?

"Something did happen, but it's not Bea or David. They're fine."

"Oh, thank, God." She frowned. "So why are you here?" She hadn't meant to sound rude, but her defenses were up.

"Could I come in to answer that question?" He, on the other hand, sounded sincere and warmhearted so of course she was going to let him in.

"Um…okay." She stepped back to allow him entry.

He seemed to fill the entire room when she closed the door. And he smelled good. And looked a little lost, like maybe he'd been feeling her absence these past few days as much as she'd felt his. But he also appeared nervous, which she'd never observed before.

He hung up his coat, motioned to the couch. At her nod, they took a seat. "I'm here because I have a Christmas gift for you."

For the first time, she noticed the small wrapped box in his hands. He handed it to her.

She accepted it, then immediately wanted to toss it back to him like this was a game of Hot Potato. Why had he gotten her a gift? What did this mean? "Shouldn't you be like thirty thousand miles up in the air right now?"

"Will you open it?" he asked in lieu of answering her.

"It's rude to answer a question with a question, you know."

He chuckled at that, insinuating she was one to talk. "Ro." His hand covered hers, and waves of tingles shot up her arm. "Please open your gift and that will hopefully answer your question."

Ro. When *he* said her name that way, it sounded like melted chocolate wrapped in silk.

Suddenly, she was terrified to unwrap the box. "I don't… I'm not sure I…" Damn it. Her voice was quivering and she didn't know the right thing to do here.

Since when do you lack guts?

"All right," she said. She tore the wrapping paper off and lifted the lid off the box. She stared at the contents, speechless, her heart in her throat, before slowly lifting the Christmas tree ornament out of the tissue paper. "*Theo.*"

The round glass bulb twinkled with tiny silver stars inside it. Written on the outside in shimmering silver and inside a tracing of a heart with an arrow through it was Theo + Rowan.

"I thought it could be our first ornament," he said, taking her free hand.

Holy silent night, was he implying what she thought he was implying?

"I love you, Rowan, and I know it's fast and we have a ton of things to work out, but you're it for me. I want a future with you and only you."

He loved her. This incredibly handsome, giving, intelligent prince loved her.

"But your family."

"Is here, too," he said, making her heart pound harder.

"I'm not a princess."

"Not yet. But you will be. When you're ready." He flashed his sexy, melt-her-bones smile.

"Your dad hates me."

He rubbed his thumb across the back of her hand. "My father is going to love you the second he meets you."

"I live here and you live in Montanique."

"One of the things we have to figure out. I'm hoping we can spend time in both places, but bottom line, my home is wherever you are. If that means relinquishing my title, then that's what I'll do."

Oh my God. Her heart was exploding with love for this man.

"I'm going to be an artist. And paint. As a career."

Theo's entire face lit up with joy. "That's fantastic. I'm happy to hear it. We could definitely use some murals around the palace." He scooted closer. "If you're not too busy with your other clients, that is."

"I think my passport's expired. Wait, I'm not even sure I have a passport."

He took the ornament out of her hand and carefully placed it back inside the box, then put the box on the coffee table. "I know how to get you one," he said quietly. Scooted even closer. "Any more obstacles you want to throw at me? Because I can handle all of them." He brushed her hair off her shoulder. "I love you. I love you so much."

She stared into his eyes. She was pretty sure she'd fallen in love with him the morning they'd first met. Damn blue eyes. "I love you, too, so much it's crazy."

"I like crazy," he said, before capturing her mouth with a kiss that made her toes curl. His lips were warm and skilled, and when he slid his tongue inside to tangle with hers, she was toast. She wrapped her arms around his neck and crawled into his lap.

"Say it again," she murmured.

"I love you."

"I love you back."

He took her face in his hands. "So is that a yes?"

"Sorry, what was the question?" She ran her fingers though his soft hair. She would never ever stop doing that.

Theo reached over and pulled the ornament out of the box. "Can we hang our first ornament on the tree?"

Our first ornament. They were an "our" now. And had hundreds of firsts in front of them.

"Absolutely."

Epilogue
Part One

The next morning…

ROWAN PULLED THE sheets up over her face. It didn't matter how much she loved listening to Theo's voice, hearing her words read aloud was weird.

Especially when he was the subject of said words and sitting next to her in bed.

Her story had made the front page of the Courier and her phone had been ringing off the hook since early this morning. Apparently, the article had already been picked up by other news media sources too. In between congrats and praise from family and friends, Theo told her without words how much he treasured her. His quiet adoration had her voicing her fondness for him quite loudly. Twice.

"Unlike a famous athlete or actor, when you're born into royalty, you don't know any different and take every day as it comes without thinking about it, the prince said. But family and private time do become your safe haven, and so spending time in Marietta with my grandparents and getting to know them and this small town has been fantastic. I'm just an ordinary person here. No special treatment. Although my grandmother seems intent on me gaining ten pounds with her delicious cooking."

Rowan smiled underneath the covers. She could tell by Theo's pause that he probably was, too.

"I've gotten to know Prince Theodore over the past few weeks and he's anything but ordinary," Theo continued, and she went back to cringing as he read her actual words. Yes, she knew he'd probably read the story, but not with her lying naked next to him! She couldn't believe how much had changed from yesterday to today. Theo was hers. Forever.

"He treats everyone he meets like they're special, and he's genuinely interested in their story. That is especially true with kids and is evident in the tireless work he does on their behalf. He says much of this inherent caring comes from his mom. When reflecting on her, Prince Theodore said he and his brother plan to do everything they can to make sure she's never forgotten. 'I hope my mother's charitable work and dedication to helping others shows in the contributions I make. She's always in my thoughts and with that, my accomplishments become hers, too.'"

Silence filled the bedroom until the newspaper rustled.

Rowan peeked out from under the sheets to find Theo staring off somewhere distant, the newspaper lowered into his lap. She sat up and put her head on his shoulder. He kissed her temple. "I know she's looking down on you and is very proud of the person you are," Ro said.

Theo tossed the newspaper to the side, turned, and had her flat on her back a second later. He braced himself on his elbows above her and smiled. She giggled. She'd been doing that a lot, happiness continually spilling out of her.

"Your article is brilliant. Thank you."

"You haven't finished reading it yet."

"I'm positive the brilliance continues." He kissed her temple, her earlobe. "I am the focus, after all," he teased before kissing her neck. Openmouthed affection continued up to her mouth where he licked her bottom lip before slipping inside to tangle their tongues.

She poured her heart and soul into the kiss.

The sound of yet another text broke them apart. As Theo reached over to check his phone, Rowan's cell chimed with a message, also. She grabbed it.

"It's Hawk," Theo said. "It appears news has spread that I missed my flight and am shacked up with you. And PS, word is we're expecting a baby."

"Not twins?" she joked. "Cassidy says, and this is all in caps, *HOW DID YOU NOT TELL ME PRINCE THEO IS STILL HERE?* Then not in caps, *ps, you're on birth control, right?*"

"I'm sorry our little bubble of bliss didn't last longer," Theo said.

"It's okay." She brushed a lock of hair off his forehead. "I'm guessing there's going to be a lot of things said about us and I'll need to ignore at least fifty percent of it."

"No second thoughts?"

"Not a one. We put an ornament up. That means you're stuck with me."

He smiled again. "There is no one else in the world I'd rather be stuck with than you, but I do have a question."

Her heart pounded. Theo hadn't officially asked her to marry him. She assumed the gift hanging on the Christmas tree pretty much did his talking, but she hoped to hear those traditional four words from him one day, and even though it was quick, now would be okay.

"Fly home with me tonight? I want you to meet my father and brother." He cupped her cheek, stared down at her with love stamped all over his handsome face. "And I hate the thought of being so far away from you."

She closed her eyes for a moment to compose herself. This was still a great question. One she wished she didn't have to say "no" to. "I can't. Christmas is in two days and my family is here. Plus, I think it might be better to sort through everything with your father without me there. I don't want to add any friction between you two. And also?" She gripped his shoulders and flipped them so she was on top. "You cannot spring a trip to Montanique on me like that! A girl needs to prepare for a meet the family and country. I can't make a first impression like the one I made on you. That would be horrible."

"Slow down there, princess. How do you know what kind of first impression you gave me?"

Rowan made her *are you for real?* face. "I think it's safe to say getting tangled in dog leashes and then having one of the dogs urinate on you ranks up there with worst first impressions ever."

"I'd classify it as most memorable. And also?" He grasped her waist and turned her over so he was back on top. "I knew right then my life would never be the same. You captivated me from the second I met you, Rowan Palotay." He kissed her softly. "And you'll captivate Montanique."

"Okay," she whispered. It was hard to argue with him when he looked at her with so much reverence in his incredible blue eyes.

"I'll miss you while I'm gone, but you're right, I should do this on my own first."

"I'll miss you, too."

He glanced over at the clock on the bedside table. "So this leaves me six hours to show you how much I love you."

She looped her arms around his neck. "I'm all yours, Your Highness."

Epilogue
Part Two

One month later…

H AWK STOPPED THEIR rented car in front of Rowan's
cottage and parked. Snow had accumulated by the
truck-full and the holiday wreath and Christmas tree were
gone from view, but everything else looked the same.

"We'll meet you up at my grandparents' house for dinner," Theo said from the passenger seat. "You'll make sure
everyone and everything is good to go?"

"I'm on it. Your grandmother has already texted me
three times. Did you really have to give her my number?"

Theo smiled. "She asked. I gave. You try saying no to
her."

"Yeah, yeah. See you soon."

"Thanks, Hawk. For everything." It had taken time to
get the king to fully embrace Theo's choices, and Hawk had
been a key voice of reason with both parties. What had
sealed the deal, however, was Rowan herself.

Theo's dad had walked in on a video chat he was having
with Rowan, and when Ro saw him in the background, she

immediately said hello. Her warm, friendly voice and disposition had the king sitting beside his son a minute later and engaged in conversation that drew genuine smiles from his father for the first time since...since Theo's mom had passed.

Theo had sat back and watched the two, his heart bursting with love for his country girl. And that was when it hit him. His father had fallen head over heels for a girl from Marietta. One conversation with Rowan, and his dad recognized something special. Something unique and beautiful, and right before Theo's eyes, his father bonded with Rowan in a way a father bonds with a daughter.

Hawk lifted his chin toward the cottage. "You're welcome. Now go get your girl."

No sooner had Theo shut the car door than the cottage door flew open and Rowan came running toward him. She leaped into his arms, her legs wrapping around his waist, her arms curving around his neck. "You're here!" she said, then latched onto his mouth like she was starved for his taste. He was certainly starved for hers.

He carried her back to the cottage while they kissed. Once inside, he kicked the door closed.

She let go, putting her feet on the floor. "Hi," she said, relieving him of his coat before taking his hand and leading him to the couch. "How was your flight?"

"It was good." He'd piloted the plane this time, with plans to fly back with Rowan as a passenger. He cupped her face in his hands. "God, I missed you." He kissed her again. They'd talked, texted, FaceTimed, or video chatted every day, but nothing compared to being with her again.

Her soft, delicate hands held his neck as she kissed him back. "Missed you more," she murmured against his lips before pulling back. "Want to see it?" she asked, beaming.

"Yes, I want to see it." Truthfully, he wanted her naked first, but she was so excited he could wait five minutes before he had his way with her.

"Don't move." She jumped to her feet, and he watched her hurry down the hallway, her backside sexier than he remembered.

Being apart had been awful, but it had given them a chance to share lengthy conversations and get to know each other even better. They'd also gotten intimate with dirty talk and naked video time. Rowan was game for anything, and thinking about it made him hard while he waited for her to return.

"Close your eyes," she called out. He closed them. "Are they closed?"

"Yes," he said.

He heard her shuffle back into the room.

"Okay, open them."

The painting Rowan held in her hands stole Theo's breath. He'd sent her a photo of himself, his father, and Otis and asked if she would paint the official royal portrait. She'd been nervous about accepting, but did it for him. "It's amazing," he said, getting to his feet. "Outstanding, incredible, perfect." He took the canvas from her and carefully set it to the side. "Just like you."

Scooping her into his arms, he carried her toward the bedroom.

"Thank you. Do you think your dad will approve?"

"I know he will. He can't wait to meet you in person, by the way."

"I'm looking forward to it, too." She put her palm on the wall, halting their momentum. "Hold up," she said playfully. "What do you think you're doing, Your Highness?"

"Taking you to bed. You're all mine for the next two hours and I plan to worship every inch of your body."

She lifted her hand. "Very well. Carry on."

He also planned to get down on one knee and ask her to marry him. He'd arranged for her parents, brother, and Cassidy to be at dinner tonight, too, so he could propose to her in front of the people who meant the most. Theo had spoken to her father a week ago to ask for her hand in marriage, and having his blessing meant a great deal.

Theo's father had something special planned for when they arrived in Montanique.

Rowan kissed the underside of his ear. "I missed your smell," she said.

"I have a cure for that." He tossed her onto the bed. She bounced. Giggled. "And will tell you all about it later, but right now, no more talking."

"Bossy Theo is kind of turning me on."

"Kind of?" He undid her jeans and pulled them down her legs.

She kicked the denim off and scooted up the bed. "Come closer and see."

After that, she quickly stripped off the rest of her clothing, he shed his, and their hands and mouths left no body part untouched.

"I love you, Ro."

"I love you, too, so, so much."

One hour and forty minutes later...

SHE SAID YES.

The End

It's going to be a royal Christmas...

Don't miss the newest royal releases!

His Jingle Bell Christmas by Barbara Dunlop

A Royal Christmas Princess by Scarlet Wilson

Christmas at the Castle by Melissa McClone

Rowan's brother Nick has his own love story.
Find out what happens in…

Falling for Her Bachelor

Available now at your favorite online retailer!

About the Author

When not attached to her laptop, USA Today Bestselling Author and RITA Finalist, Robin Bielman loves to read, take hikes with her hubby, and frequent coffee shops. A California girl, the beach is her favorite place for fun, relaxation, and inspiration.

She loves to go on adventures, and has skydived, scuba dived, parasailed, gotten lost in the wilderness (and only suffered a gazillion bug bites for it) hiked to waterfalls, and swam with dolphins. In her spare time she also tries to put her treadmill to good use while watching her favorite TV shows, indulges her sweet tooth, and plays a mean game of sock tug of war with her cute, but sometimes naughty dog, Harry.

Writing is a dream come true, and she still pinches herself to be sure it's real. She lives in Southern California with her high school sweetheart husband and loves to connect with readers.

Get the scoop on Robin, her books, and sign up for her newsletter on her website at robinbielman.com

Thank you for reading

Once Upon a Royal Christmas

If you enjoyed this book, you can find more from all our
great authors at TulePublishing.com, or from your favorite
online retailer.

Made in United States
North Haven, CT
28 November 2024

61101394R00145